RUN-OUT GROOVE

Joseph Coward

Published 2023 by the87press

The 87 Press LTD

87 Stonecot Hill

Sutton

Surrey

SM3 9HJ

www.the87press.co.uk

ISBN: 978-1-7399547-9-6

Printed and bound by CPI Group (UK) Ltd, Croydon, CR0 4YY

Design: Stanislava Stoilova [www.sdesign.graphics]

For Alex, my life

PART ONE

1.

Here follows a thin and mediocre volume of verse.

I was born a boy covered in my own shit, then I got wiped clean and handed to my mother, in hospital. I was small, and then I got bigger. I had two parents, and three sisters, one older, two younger, called One, Two and Three, in whichever order you prefer to imagine. The house where we lived was sat in post-industrial Essex in 1991, the year I showed up, the place and time to be if you liked pebble-dashed housing, and casual queer bashing.

My Mum and Dad stayed together til I was mostly done growing up, but when I think back to what I observed of their marriage through childish eyes, maybe I wish now that they hadn't waited so long to call it quits. She was twenty-one when she married Dad, who was thirty-one. To the best of my knowledge he never nagged her, she never hit him, they never openly fought, but there was something in the way, some great gap where communication ought to have been, an obstacle that they were unable even to name, much less overcome. Could've been their age difference. Could've been Dad's impossible-to-deal-with deafness that made even the briefest of conversations with him painful beyond a mere chore (working a knackered old bookbinding machine had robbed him of most of his hearing). Could've been Mum's paranoia at having married so young; perhaps writing her name at the registry office felt like signing her own death warrant.

I think my sisters and I were a constant, shrill reminder of her rash decision to give up so much of her life so young, or maybe the result of it, or maybe we compounded that particular unhealing, somewhat self-inflicted wound. When she was especially exasperated at our constant scrapping Mum would screech, clutching with desperation at frayed sleeves for something, anything to hold on to, "when you're older you're only going to have unhappy memories of your childhood!" She was right, about mine at least, but not for the reason she thought; we were unhappy because she was unhappy. She radiated misery for as long as I knew her. Never knew what dad felt about anything.

Anyway the two of them sat it out until they reached their respective forty-fifth and fifty-fifth years, and probably mortality was looming larger in their minds than before, and they couldn't take the ringing silence anymore. One day Mum stopped talking to us, then she stopped sleeping in the same bed as Dad, and then one day she was gone. She took up with someone else, some tradesman or something, and he was a cunt and he took her for every penny of her divorce money before he beat her to death. Marry in haste, repent at leisure – that's something people say. Mum didn't get much repenting time, though I'm not sure what sin she was supposed to have committed in the first place.

•

One early memory I have of Dad is him mocking my handwriting when I was four. Probably I'd learned to write not long before that, and I would write down the J at the start of my name backwards so that it looked like an oversized lowercase L, and he saw it and crowed, "hello Lude," in a sing-song voice, and his cackling face seemed to loom closer while the room shrank away, like a dolly zoom, or a dream. His face was red. We were in the hall. I protested, probably insisted that my way of writing my own name was correct, which only intensified his teasing. And then my memory of this event fades, like the tide rushing away, if it ever happened at all. I read somewhere that we only remember something once, and after that we're only remembering the memory. Anyway I knocked my Dad unconscious for the first time when I was fourteen.

It was deepest winter, the light inside seemed yellow and the windows were opaquely black, and the TV radiated warmth and there was electric hum, carpet smell. Dad came home from work under a thundercloud, and before he'd got his coat off, Mum, with expert bad timing, went to him with news of my having been a little shit to my sisters all evening. Which I had been, was always being, but without pause Dad dragged me away from Newsround by my neck, and threw me to the living room floor. I shrieked in surprise, and then he fell upon me in a rage, one knee either side of my head as I lay on my back, closed fists raining blows on my chest and face. Then somehow I wriggled free and I was on my feet, and we stood opposite each other, panting and squinting with bared teeth, arms akimbo like gunslingers, or territorial male monkeys. There was a brief beat with flashing eyes and then he swung for me again but missed, and then I swung back and his jaw ricocheted off my knuckles, quick then slow like a party balloon, and he drifted, deflated, to the ground.

Mum came running at the loud thunk he made as he fell, and he was stirring by the time she had rushed to crouch by his side. Her body angled towards his, she turned her head and looked at me with a look of hatred and fear that said "today has finally happened." I went to my room and shut the door, and sat with my back to it til the next morning, fully clothed and hungry and barely breathing, not making a sound.

That was the first of many fights Dad and I had over the next two years. At the mildest provocation of one by the other, chairs would be overturned and dinner trays upended and we'd be glumly trading dumb blows in the middle of the living room floor while the heads of One, Two and Three stacked up on top of each other in a doorway, each of them open-mouthed and wet-tongued, wondering what this time in all our lives meant for them.

We had our last fight when I was sixteen. I made some comment as I walked away from an argument and he punched me in the back of the head, and I staggered forwards and turned and punched him back, landing a right-handed jab on his nose. He shrieked and clasped his hands to his face and I saw blood oozing from between his fingers, and then Mum did something she hadn't done before. Instead of going to Dad's aid, glowering at me over her shoulder as she tended to whatever retaliative wound I'd inflicted, she surged towards me and pushed her face into mine, and snarled, in a voice I'd never heard come from her mouth before: "get out of our house."

Then with strange strength, she marched me to the back door and threw me into the alley. Freezing rain had been pissing down all day and I gasped in diving reflex as my unshoed socked feet hit icy water, and as the back door slammed behind me I was left with no choice but to walk, and keep walking. The rain still came down and "get out of our house" rang in my ears, and the world outside was a wilderness and I walked uphill on my own like an exorcised ghost.

I went to Rip's house, and his parents let me stay the night without asking any questions, and they gave me fresh socks and a pair of trainers to wear to school the next day. Instead of going to registration the next morning I knocked at the Head of Year's office, and he let me in and somehow knew everything without me saying a word. He said I'd have to write down what happened, a statement, he called it. Mum called the school and they gave the phone to me and she cried down the line, about how I might have made it so my sisters would be taken away from her. The Head of Year listened to my side of the exchange, and I could feel him looking at me with sad wonder. The Deputy Headmaster came to look at what I'd written, and he read it and said "is this your handwriting?" and I said yes and he replied "how beautiful."

•

"They checked for me bruises at school, you know," Number One told me, ages afterwards.

"What do you mean?" I said.

"After you told on Dad, they took me to the San, and the Matron and the Head of Year made me take my clothes off and looked at me in my underwear, to see if he'd hit me as well."

"But he hadn't, though."

"No."

"Or Two, or Three."

"No."

"Wonder why," I said.

"Dunno," she said.

2.

I went back home that day after school and what had happened was never spoken of again, but Dad and I didn't fight anymore. To replace the humdrum violence, I set about destroying my education: I repeatedly truanted and smoked fags openly and antagonised my teachers with bored wit, and didn't turn up to take any exams, and so I got chucked out. Then they made me go to a sixth form college to at least attempt some A-levels. I knew Mum and Dad didn't care what I did, but I guessed they had to at least be seen to be doing something. I ended up begrudgingly getting on with my studies at college, at least at first, because Rip was already enrolled there, and I thought that even if the entire experience was as hateful as I expected it to be, we'd at least have each other's company. I did ultimately fuck up my education, through a kind of persistent negligence, but I don't know if any of the adults who were supposed to be in charge of me particularly noticed, or cared. It had all got to that sort of stage.

Anyway I would knock for Rip at his parents' house every school morning, and he and I would walk to college together. We'd go down Shenfield's shambolic and semi-abandoned high street, which served only commuters and other passers-through, and its air was fusty with a thin, brown-carpeted smell of boredom. One such morning a low mist clung to the ground and swirled at our ankles and it dampened the sounds of the street, and no one was around. We stopped by a cafe and Rip bought us a cup of coffee each, which we both took black. The morning was empty and still.

We turned a corner and passed a construction site, and a builder placed two fingers in his mouth and wolf-whistled at Rip.

"Piss off," Rip spat over his shoulder, without breaking pace. The builder seemed satisfied with telling us he'd fuck (or maybe had already fucked) our mothers, and then sloped off behind some scaffolding. I looked at Rip in the corner of my eye and he said nothing, just stared coolly ahead, blowing air across the rim of his styrofoam cup. I felt bad that he had got used to this: he had immediate plans to demolish his outer womanly façade but while he waited for planning permission, various shit eaters like the builder often mistook him for a girl, and treated him as they would treat all beings they regarded as inferior to themselves.

"It's insane that I get treated like less of a man than you," Rip said with a snarling smirk, as we walked, "it's a fucking joke."

"You're more of a man than I could ever be, Euripides," I said, in my best fainting Bond girl voice. I always said this, and it always earned me a dead arm, and a "fuck you, fag."

I'd first met Rip a few years before at some bullshit

inter-school event, where about a thousand kids were ferried into a freezing auditorium to endure skits performed by out-of-work actors, reciting scripts peppered with outdated slang, telling us about the evils of drugs or how to fuck in the right position, or whatever. I had slipped off after an interval and planned to walk round and round the building until the sorry afternoon was over, when I saw Rip leaning on a Coke machine in the lobby. He had a shaved head and was wearing the uniform of the girls' school he was made to attend, with the bearing of somebody just doused with freezing water. We looked at each other across chlorine-smelling space and I can't remember who spoke to who first but it was nice and kind, and then he was walking round and round the building with me. He told me about his bad school, and how he was finally getting out. Drab as Shenfield Sixth Form College was, it was to be something of an escape for him. People there wouldn't know him by another name, he said.

We spent the rest of the walk to college badmouthing the catcalling builder, hoping that between now and the end of the day some loose masonry would fall and crush his skull.

The other kids at Shenfield were OK. They were mostly from lower-middle-class families like mine, about half white, quarter black, quarter Asian, keeping political identities and general queerness, or lack of it, to themselves. I took this as a sign that I should do the same, and Rip seemed in tacit agreement with me. People probably thought that he and I were fucking or something, but if they did they kept that to themselves too, so I didn't really care. Like me, some of them had been chucked out by former secondary schools; some were pursuing the more idiotic courses offered by the college, like Travel and Tourism, or How to Sit Down and Stay There, or whatever. They were perplexed by Rip and gave him a wide berth, and because of our association they ignored me. Rip liked being thought of as mysterious; I felt weird being invisible.

We trudged through the gates, past the sign that said *"SHENFIELD SIXTH FORM COLLEGE: Security, Business, Success"*, over the gravel drive and past rows of teachers in the carpark stepping heavily in unison from their Mondeos, Sharans, Galaxies, '98 Volvo Sedans, Escorts, Peugeot 206s, Sierras, Nissan Sunnys and Subarus; into the entrance hall where to the left of us there was an iron-curtained food hatch through which, in a few hours' time, forlorn slices of pizza would be pushed in exchange for a quid that might be (and usually was) better spent at the arcade by the kids who could somehow always forego food as long as they were dosed up on enough nicotine, and then we went into the chilly corridor that took us inexorably every Monday to our first class of the week.

I had no real interest in English, and would have preferred to take music or tech courses, anything that didn't involve a ton of reading and writing, but I thought my survival hinged on sticking close to Rip, so I made sure I was in all his classes. I was currently regretting my decision to be in this particular class, though, because we were having to read *Wuthering Heights*, a book by a miserable Victorian about miserable rich people being miserable cunts to each other. Some people apparently thought it was a love story.

Rip and I entered the classroom and dallied to our seats at the centre of the desk horseshoe which faced the blackboard, dumping our bags and sitting down, peering out from under our brows at our classmates, who clicked greasily at their phones and ignored us.

In the pre-class hubbub I was lamenting the reemergence of an old childhood acquaintance, Sean, the son of a friend of Mum's. I hadn't seen him since the age of about twelve, but he'd recently got hold of my mobile number and kept texting me to invite me to dinners, birthdays, and other bullshit that involved dressing up way past my level of tolerance for that sort of thing, and putting on super-straight airs for him and his posh mates. Rip asked who he was again and I said "y'know, the rich prick I used to know, who lives on some mentally massive estate past the common. I've got to go back there for some other party."

"Ah yes," Rip said, "dickhead revisited."

"Morning everyone," said our teacher as I spat coffee down my shirt and Rip boomed with laughter and Mrs Whoever told us to settle down as she bustled into the room preceded by a teetering armload of files and papers and a mug of hot liquid precariously pinched by a spare finger and thumb. "Please have your Brontës *out*–" ("get your Brontës out for the lads" someone sang under their breath) "–and be ready to read to the class, thank you." This was why Rip and I always sat in the centre of the desk horseshoe: there was no telling from which direction our handler would command Monday's faltering flow of reading to begin, so if we sat in the middle at the back of the room, there'd always be at least twelve or so kids before us, and it usually meant the lesson would end before we were made to read.

Thirty chilly students reluctantly hunched over battered copies of *Wuthering Heights*. I began to slightly panic as the teacher breezed through five, six, seven readers and I was not far off having to stumble through the boring prose myself. When I was one classmate away from having to squeak out Victorian dialogue which I neither understood nor gave the first shit about, I was saved by Catherine, a girl with a great knack for asking the most irrelevant and stupid questions thinkable, but always at a time that brilliantly halted the progress of the class. She said something like, how could Brontë have been so inspired despite being ill all the time, and maybe the coldness of the moors was a lack of love, and then she asked if Hindley was beating up Heathcliff because he was racist. Some students were obviously itching for their turn to read and their internal groan at the crap she was coming out with was almost audible, but I revelled in the delay. The bell rang, and I sighed with relief.

Books and papers fluttered upwards like startled birds as everyone stood, and there was a chorus of screeching chairs. The teacher said something over the din but it was lost in the noise, and the door was banging open and closed as the class trudged glumly to their next lesson.

"Fucking great," Rip sighed to himself as he got to his feet, and dropped his books back into his bag.

"What?" I said.

"Bleeding," he said out of the side of his mouth.

"Gross," I said, "do you have a–"

"Nope," he said. "Lucky I didn't don my virginal white robes today, innit?"

"Sorry, your *vaginal*–?"

"Virginal!" he barked, and the people still trailing out of class looked back at us and laughed. We waited until we were the last ones in the room, and then left too.

3.

In the summer of 2010 I felt myself drifting strangely, but I couldn't help it. I was nearing the end of living with Mum and Dad and their marriage seemed washed up, and One and Two had moved away, One to live with a boyfriend and study overseas, Two somewhere else, and I could feel the last dregs of our family draining away.

I failed to complete my studies at Shenfield, and opted instead to undertake extensive research in booze and the effects of it, and the result of my experiment was that I spent much of year thirteen very fucked up indeed. Rip didn't drink because he got Asian flush but he'd still often bunk off with me over the fields behind Brentwood's old Alms Houses, and stick his nose into a book while I drank myself stupid and sang at the clouds. When Dad found out about this final ruination of my education, he screamed at me without let-up for a day, for my "pigheadedness … arrogance … waste of a brain"; but after that he basically ignored the situation – and me – until I left for good not long after.

One afternoon Rip and I were sat opposite each other, cross-legged with our knees touching, on the floor of my bedroom. Golden light came in slowly through the interstices of the blinds covering my window, and red hot dust motes danced in it. We passed a fag back and forth. Smoke lazily curled from my lip and rose to the ceiling, disappearing. The neck of my shitty old acoustic guitar was lain across Rip's right thigh as we sorted through the pile of vinyl records he and I had amassed by pooling scant savings, and trawling the one surviving record shop in our town over the past however long. I'd started the record collection after going through Mum's old albums, through her discovering Neil Young and Patti Smith, and David Bowie and Lizzie Mercier Descloux. I'd looked them up online to devour every piece of information on them that I could find, plundering the bottomless well of "Associated Acts" links on Wikipedia, and making lists on reams of paper of the records I would covet, but for months be unable to buy. I think everything I listened to was based on those early discoveries, connecting to a shivering thread that still clung to the first moment I heard Neil sing "*look at mother nature on the run in the 1970s.*"

My favourite single and prized possession was an original Teenage Jesus and the Jerks seven-inch called "Orphans", which showed me at fifteen the crazy way music could be played when you got rid of ideas like convention, and talent. The run-out groove inscription read "*make me a real bloody Bloody Mary.*" I stuck it on. Lydia Lunch howled over ear-splitting, formless guitar and pounding drums:

Little orphans running through the bloody snow
Little orphans running through the bloody snow
Little orphans running through the blood
Through the blood
Through the blood

"Do you ever worry," Rip said, inhaling a lungful of smoke and passing the dog-end of the cigarette to me, to kill, "that there isn't enough time to listen to everything? Like, do you get anxious about missing out on all the good music there is?"

"Not really," I said, gazing over the foot-high stack of singles and LPs that we shared, and that I housed. "It's more like... there's loads of shit out there, so how do you avoid all the shit? You know?"

"Maybe. But even if you wanted to hear all the stuff that you knew you'd like, or that everyone told you was good, it just doesn't feel like there's time." I picked up the guitar from Rip's lap and knocked out a few clumsy chords.

"I think there's time." I crushed the fag butt on the edge of a nearby near-empty coke bottle, and dropped it inside, where it extinguished with a hiss.

No more ankles and no more clothes
Little orphans running through the snow
Little orphans in the blood in the blood in the blood

We sat in silence as the record played out, and let it keep spinning after it finished. Rip's mobile buzzed on the carpet next to him. He flipped it open, and read the text message he'd received. "Oh" he said and I said "what" and he didn't reply and I paused and said "what" again, and he told me that his friend Marta had invited him to their club night in London. My only experience of gigs had been shows at Brentwood's Seaxe

Bar, which was attached to the crumbling Essex Arms, and at which toothless cover bands played dilapidated versions of chart hits, from ages ago. I'd never been to a real London show.

"What sort of thing is it?" I said.

"Not sure," Rip said, already tapping out his reply to Marta. "A few bands I know, Wet Dog, Bastard Sword, Rayographs. One I've never heard of. Could be good."

"You're gonna go?"

"Might. Wanna come?"

"Sure."

We went. I'd barely been to London, despite living on its outskirts my entire life. School trips there were a thing, but I was never interested: the stinking coaches you used to have to take to get there made me feel sick. So when Rip and I alighted from a DLR train and descended the steps at Shadwell Station, I gulped excitement from the ashy air and felt it settle like sediment at the bottom of my gut. The George Tavern, where the night's show was to be held, was just around the corner.

The day had been hot and the night was becoming cold. We stood at the side of the road waiting at the lights, facing the place. The man went green and we crossed. We paid five quid on entering through the pub's side door: my fiver ready in my hand, and thrust into the palm of a thin pale kid, with big hair and dark rings around his eyes; Rip had to fish in his pocket for the right change before he got let in. The kid taking the money (he was probably around the same age as me and Rip) gave us a withering look, up and down, as we entered. I'd taken lately to wearing a kurta, black but quickly faded grey in too-hot washes, tight jeans and Doc Martens that were at least a size too big for me; Rip had taken to calling me a goth parasol. He was wearing, and also always wore, an acid-washed denim jacket and wraparound mirrored shades. Our outfits made us look strange enough separately, and absurd together. We didn't look anything like the rest of the people in the bar, who seemed all to be dressed in barely-varied understated monochrome: Ben Shermans, vintage sheepskins, those tasselled little loafers before anyone called them 'tom shoes', broad-brimmed hats, stiff overcoats, print dresses, big boot and military jacket combos, an orchestra of dangling earrings. One or two of the more adventurous among them affected a tie or something, but colour-wise they all pretty much looked like they were wearing a kind of bizarro business-casual. It was only seven thirty but the pub was full, and the crowd was roaring over the music which was deejayed in a cramped corner by another big haired kid, who was holding a big set of headphones to one ear while flipping idly through a metal case of seven-inches. All the pub's mismatched and beaten-up furniture was pointed towards the centre of the room, where a makeshift stage had been set up.

Rip and I meekly made for the bar. A fierce looking woman who I would later know as Helen, the pub landlady, was serving. I ordered Rip a coke and asked for a lager for myself. Helen's eyes flicked briefly upwards to meet mine, and she slammed back the arm of the beer machine with the bearing of a person compelled to live among animals. When my glass was full she banged it onto the bar in front of me. I paid five pounds sixty altogether for our drinks and turned while lifting my cup close to my chin to lean my back against the bar and face the room. I pursed my lips in restorative silence around the edge of the glass.

"Oh, there's Marta," Rip said, digging me in the ribs. From across the room a girl was waving at Rip. She came over and the two of them hugged.

"I'm Jude," I said, when they had said muffled hellos into each others' shoulders, and parted. I offered Marta a hand and she took it lightly, gripping the tips of my fingers with the tips of hers. She was tall and slim and glamorous, and looked at me with vague dislike.

"Jude and I went to school together," Rip said, contextualising me, and with his eyes saying to Marta "he's OK." She blinked and brushed a strand of her long auburnish hair behind one ear. She must have been twenty-three, twenty-four. Half-turning to me, Rip went on, "Marta and I first met in that group I told you about, and then we met in person at a show this year." I nodded and said I remembered. Marta asked us if we had drinks and we said we were OK. There was a pause which I filled by saying "I like your dress" to Marta and she smiled with an eyebrow cocked, and said "I like yours too." I blushed and clamped my pint glass to my face.

Rip asked Marta how the night was going and she sighed "fine," adding, "haven't done one here in ages." Then she gestured to the crowd, saying, "same old people, then again I must have put on this same line-up about two dozen times."

"Great bands though," said Rip, chewing at his straw. "I'm looking forward to Rayographs. Haven't seen them yet."

"It's just Astrid, the singer, tonight," Marta said. "The drummer couldn't do it, or something, so she's playing solo. She should be playing... now, actually."

The DJ shut off the music at that moment and the lights went down and everybody's heads turned towards the centre of the room. The crowd parted, and through it and onto the area of floor acting as the stage stepped a girl of about twenty-two, adorned in a purple sequinned wrap dress, with a light grey shawl slung around her shoulders. Her long black hair was in her eyes as she bent to pick up a guitar, it was a red twelve-string and on the headstock was painted the legend "Orpheus". She stepped into crude stage light to reveal her face, which was beautiful. She had black-rimmed eyes and a hard look full of purpose and someone at the back yelled "yeeeeoow" and there was a buzz as her guitar got plugged in, and then she stepped up to the microphone and began to play.

I guess until about that moment I'd always somehow assumed that only the music of the past was real and worth something, and that nothing new could be good, maybe because of the way Mum had always talked about the seventies like they were fucking Xanadu or something. But this, this was really real: Astrid's songs were sad and elegantly flowing, her fingers picking out complex rhythms on the twelve-string while her clarinet-like voice sailed stoically over the top of them, and her eyes fluttered and her mouth made weird shapes to release notes which leaped and bounded from one octave to another, and her feet were in fourth position and her words danced and the room was silent and swayed in time to her mesmeric music, and I swayed on the spot.

Rip appeared at my side and placed a drink into my hand, taking my empty glass away from me. The new one frothed and overflowed and I slopped beer down my front, and I nodded at Rip in dumb thanks and continued to watch Astrid's performance in a state of unblinking awe as the music wound itself around me. She didn't pause or speak between songs, which became frenetic and jagged in the middle of the set before dwindling to whispers at its end; she only once allowed for applause, and started each new song before the audience knew the one before it had ended. Her fearsome approach to this acousmatic, punkish folk made my eyes burn in their sockets, and I felt something stir inside me, like the glower of an ember beneath a pile of ash.

During her final song which had a jaunty and marching rhythm, a lyric jumped out at me that went:

> As all around me sleeps,
> A sad song weeps: 'Love is so hard to keep'

and it rattled around in my head masking all the other words in the piece until its finale, which was a ringing chord and the words *"all roads lead to you,"* delivered on a single, sultry breath.

The set ended, and the room erupted. Astrid stepped back from the microphone to take a bow as the audience's whistles sailed over her head. She smiled and took her leave through the crowd which parted again for her, then closed around her as she left the stage, swallowing her up as if she'd been a dream of mine. I told myself not to follow her yet.

Rip and I began talking immediately about the show, quickly batting opinions back and forth, and I could tell he hadn't liked it as much as me, like, he agreed with me, but soon instead of saying anything he kept on saying "mmhm" to everything I said, and then was looking furtively around the room, probably for Marta who I suspected he wanted to fuck. I decided to leave him to it and pushed my way through Astrid's crowd, which did not part for me, and made my way outside to smoke.

In the garden I saw Astrid leaning with her back to the pub's brick wall, limp-wristedly cradling a cigarette in one hand. She looked up as I stepped outside and our eyes met and I did that purse-mouthed, hi-I-don't-know-you smile, and she did one back at me. Stutteringly I said I loved her performance and she thanked me. She had sunk into a large leopard print coat, and looked very fabulous in it. I mentioned the song with the lyric I liked, starting to stammer it back to her and she half-laughed and said thank you over the tail end of my sentence, politely drowning out my over-earnesty. No one else was in the garden with us. She asked me if I played as well, and I said "a little guitar" and she said "oh," and crushed her fag underfoot, saying as she left, "it was nice to meet you."

The rest of the night passed in a fair haze. I got drunk on about eight pints and some shots, Rip and I ended up bouncing around together in a makeshift moshpit to Wet

Dog's set, limbs flailing to their threadbare beat and beer going up in the air, and then the big lights were on and people were filing out and Rip and Marta were kissing, and in the mirror in the toilets I saw my face had greased over and I'd had a great time, but then I was glad to go.

Rip and I stared at our washed out reflections in the train carriage window on the way back, making faces at each other, tiredly nuzzling into each other's necks and leaning on each other's shoulders and I blinked and we were pulling into Brentwood station, and I blinked and I was bent over the sink at Mum and Dad's house, puking, and I woke up the next morning to Rip smoking out of my window and my hair was sat in shock on top of my head and he turned to me and grinned, and I grinned with pain back at him.

4.

The summer ended. I got a job working in that same coffee shop that Rip and I used to go to every day before school, while Rip opted to take a year off before going to King's College in London, where he'd been accepted to study Philosophy. He was enduring endless teasing from me because I was jealous. The one joke I used to do that really got him going was nonsensically saying that studying philosophy made him a class traitor, and I'd always have to duck as he unfailingly swung for me every time I said it. He never connected once, but I was fast because I'd had practise. We were both saving up to move out of Essex in the next few months, and I couldn't wait to get away.

My shifts were OK. I worked about thirty hours a week. I'd learned how to make coffee, which was something. My boss told me "you'll have a job any time, any place in the world if you can make a good cup of coffee." Sadly I thought he was right.

•

I had tried for several weeks after Astrid's show, on the floor of my bedroom, legs crossed, to write a song. I felt as though I knew that the key to doing it was just to do it, and I was trying, but nothing was forthcoming. I felt like I had nothing to write about.

I thought about Astrid singing *"all roads lead to you"* and what I could do with that, yet still nothing came. I screwed my eyes shut and suspended the pen above the paper and urged words to come. Still nothing.

One afternoon while I was sitting there doing this, this nothing, Dad came stomping down the landing and bashed his knuckles on my bedroom door as he passed, and my eyes snapped open. Suddenly I had it. There I went. The pen came alive in my hand and in my own unpractised scrawl and cradling my old guitar in my lap, my tongue sticking out the side of my mouth, I wrote:

> *My father's fist struck hot*
> *Like an insect bite*
> *And as I walked through freezin rain*
> *I thought: put on some shoes*
> *Put on an accent*
> *Move to London*
> *And so it was that I took the pill*
> *I took the Tube down to Mile End*
> *Danny came home with wet socks*
> *It was a chillin reminder*
> *I'm not so far from home*

I scribbled "FREEZIN RAIN" at the top of the page and it was the first start to a song I had ever written. It was the only time I'd written about that night since I'd been made to put it in a statement for those school officials, since the day after Dad and I traded blows for the last time, since the day I'd been told that my sisters could be taken away because of me. I was not far away from turning nineteen.

My eyes roved over the page. I hummed out some sounds and started mimicking them with the guitar: big, bashed clams of major chords that flirted with discord and churned repeatedly, structureless but suggesting melody that might move lightly, which was unpredictable and good. With no real singing style to speak of, I tried on for size a shout that followed the chords exactly. It came up from my gut and was simple, but with a tremulous quality that was mine, and a warm weight felt lifted on a rope from the bottom of my stomach, to glow like a coal in my chest.

"It's really good," Rip said, when I played it to him a week later. He spilled ash from his cigarette onto the "Freezin Rain" lyric sheet which by now I'd typed out to show him.

"Yeah?" I said, shaking the ash off the page, which I smoothed out on carpet.

"Yes! It's so, like, I dunno, and I love how there's no verse-chorus-verse thing going on, it sounds great." I mumbled thank you into the hollow of my crossed legs.

"I think I'm going to work on it some more," I said, "maybe come up with a longer intro or something, maybe a solo."

"No, keep it as it is," Rip said, smiling. "It's a good length, too." I resisted the urge to half-joke that he was saying it was a good length because it was so short. "But you know what this means, though," he went on. I waited. "It means," he said, "you will soon have to make your shining and glorious debut."

"I fucking will not," I said. "No way, no thanks." We laughed but I knew he was right, and I wanted to. There was a beat as I thought about the meaning of it all.

"Who's Danny?" Rip asked me, looking at the lyrics.

"I made it up, him up, I mean," I said, with an indifferent-sounding sniff. "I just thought that something like that could happen, someone walking outside with no shoes."

"Right on," Rip said, not remembering.

I felt a very small joy that grew inside of me and I cultivated it shyly, and every time I served a cup of coffee or stood listlessly at the shop's back door smoking fags, apron on, I smiled at the thought that I had something that no one knew about yet. And I wanted them to know, and that desire kept me going all through September and October and into the winter as the nights got darker.

5.

The incised skin on my forearm sprang apart like an overstretched canvas ripping, white parting, revealing red, and I gasped as rosebuds of blood winked through the wound I'd made. I put the bread knife down. Its teeth were smeared mauve from the bite it had taken out of my flesh. Early morning sunshine wandered through the garden into the kitchen, freckling through leaves onto the counter in front of me. I spun in surprise as Mum clattered a cup and saucer in the next room: I didn't know she was there, how long had she been there?

"Fuck," I breathed, turning aimlessly this way and that, on the spot, "fuck." Padding sticky-footed on linoleum I snapped off a piece of kitchen towel from the roll, placed it flat on my arm, letting the drying blood stick the paper to my skin, and yanked down my shirtsleeve over the makeshift bandage. I breathed in as I walked through the kitchen door and then breathed heavily out again, adjusting to the pressure of the dining room, like a diver descending.

I silently said good morning and sat next to Mum at

the table. It was the first time we'd sat like this in a month, more than that. She took her meals through to the other room these days, not even to watch TV, just to sit on her own. She had stopped cooking for us, and so Dad did it disastrously for a bit before I started to think of things I could make, and we sat eating my experiments in silence every night while her presence thrummed heavily in the room next door.

This morning she was in her pyjamas, puffy-eyed and staring into her cup, and I wondered if the fact that she wasn't wearing the clothes from the day before meant she'd slept in the same bed as Dad last night. I saw her head turn nearly imperceptibly in the corner of my eye, and then I heard her snuffle and realised she had started to cry. Glassy beads of tears ran to her cheeks and fell, making little *thok* sounds as they struck the dining room table. I couldn't speak, and I found the sight of her weeping weirdly alien, a somehow obscene act, and I felt frightened and repelled.

"Jude," Mum said, thickly through crying, "what have you done?" I looked down to see mauve blossoming like watercolour on my shirtsleeve, and clamped a hand over it and thought fuck, and hurriedly said "I don't remember."

"I don't know what I'm going to do," Mum said, looking away from me, and then she said it again as she began to tremble, and then confess strange things to me, words I wanted to obliterate by screaming.

I closed my eyes and when I opened them she was gone, and then closed them again, and then opened them again, and Dad was standing over me and I jumped, banging my knees hard on the dining room table.

"You're up early," he said, too loud, and I looked slowly up at him and he looked down at me and said, "you've got blood on your shirt."

•

On the first of December, Rip and I moved into a place together. I'd turned nineteen three days before. Rip presented me with a Sarah Kane book as a present, my only one that year. I'd heard of Kane because she'd gone to Shenfield, but never read or seen her stuff. It was the first book I put on the shelf that came with my new room.

From my job I had managed to scrape away about six hundred quid in savings, and Rip's parents had hooked him up with a deposit and guarantees and everything else we needed. I wasn't sorry to say goodbye to Brentwood; my parents didn't say much about my leaving and I didn't see Dad for the longest time after that. I never saw Mum again. I'd like to be able to write that there was some kind of dramatic reckoning between Dad and me, but it didn't happen that way. Number Three gave me a card in which she wrote "good luck" but didn't sign – on the front there was a picture of a hot air balloon sailing over a sunny field, with a country house pictured far in the distance.

The flat Rip and I found was the ground floor of a terraced house in Stepney Green, only twenty-odd miles from where I'd spent my whole life but it felt like another planet to me. I was not grown up and I had not seen the world. Women covered by full religious dress on crowded pavements surprised me; I was never asked for ID in bars, and there were bars everywhere. Anyway I jacked in my job at home and got a new one at another coffee place on our new street, and Rip had some savings from ages ago that he got as inheritance from an uncle who'd died, and so didn't have to work yet. He'd be finding something whenever, and in the first few weeks of our tenancy he often said that he was looking for something he'd like to do. I'd never thought of work like that. I was doing forty hours a week with early starts, and coming home in the late afternoons to write music.

We threw a housewarming party. I didn't know anyone and so I leaned on Rip to invite as many of his London pals who I also knew, trying to limit the number of strangers in my new home, which I was still getting to know.

On the day of the party, Rip set about buying things and dragging the dinner table along the kitchen floor to a far wall, to set up a place for drinks and stuff. His booze selection was both weird and terrible, bad red wine alongside a single bottle of some liqueur I'd never even heard of, and no mixer. There wasn't enough of anything apart from crisps, and I gave him shit for it and he told me to go and buy stuff myself, then, since I knew so fucking much.

"Thank God for me," I said, hefting onto the table a case of Holsten Pils and a small bottle of Glenn's, and some orange juice. I only slightly resented his ability to spend money on booze while unemployed, and spending any money at all on friends who weren't mine, but I relished the thought of the bottle of bourbon that was stashed under my bed, for me.

"Yeah, yeah," Rip said as our doorbell rang for the first time, and he went to greet a guest. On the step were three boyish men I'd never met, dressed in darkish paisley and not looking at me when Rip brought them in to say hello. They helped themselves to the beers I'd bought, and stood leaning against the kitchen counter, sipping in silent unison, and I laughed inwardly as they all stared at the same invisible spot on the ceiling, clearly regretting being the first ones to arrive.

By eleven thirty the twenty or so people Rip had invited had all come, with about twenty of their friends. My turntable which was kept in the living room had been commandeered by a trio of girls with matching beehived hair and caked foundation, and I was glad when my own record collection was deemed acceptable, and no one tried to put on tunes of their own.

Marta came too, out of her dress from a few months

before and into a playsuit but with the same high heels I noticed, and her auburn hair was coiled high on top of her head. She came up to me and kissed me on the cheek and looked into my eyes and smiled and said hello, then went away and talked to some other people she knew but who I didn't know.

More people came. Someone gave me some coke. I remembered having told Rip over a year ago that I'd done it already, like I knew he did on his rare days off from me, but actually I'd never done it and was scared I didn't know how. But then Marta was in on it, and waving under my sinuses a CD case with a fat line of white powder on it, and we were in Rip's bedroom with Rip and Marta and a cute boy and I had three pairs of eyes expectantly on me, so I just took the note Marta gave me and snorted it all up, resisting the powerful urge to puke as it dripped from my nose to the back of my throat.

I tilted my head back and tried not to react, and everybody laughed and then I coughed and laughed, then everything did its thing and I was suddenly high, this was being high. It was different to being drunk, and then I wanted to be more drunk. (I looked at the cute boy and he had no name and his eyes grew, and I suddenly felt numb all over and wanted to laugh, and be his everything, I felt good, I felt OK, this was good, this was OK.)

We stayed there a long while, getting higher as the party thumped in the walls around us. Rip and Marta coiled around each other on his bed. The four of us stared at one another in anticipation of someone saying something, anything, so that we could enthuse too, say things that perhaps were true but that we'd hate ourselves for, only a few hours later (I didn't know about that bit yet). I kept thinking this is it, maybe everything will be good and in this room forever. Then Rip said he had to go for a piss and unwound himself from Marta and left the room with a creak of the bed, and then I realised dumbly that the cute boy had left already.

"So," said Marta.

"So," I said.

"Rip tells me," she said, and burped, "that you play music."

"Oh," I said, surprised. I burped too, in sympathy. "I'm trying to write some songs–"

"Let's hear one," she said.

"My guitar's in my–"

"Let's go to your room and get it," she said.

So we got up and went. I sat down on my bed and she sat down close by me. She passed me my own guitar, dumping it heavily into my lap. "Play," she said.

Bug-eyed and with the new feeling of coke still shaking through my veins, I started up "Freezin Rain". There was nothing but my scratching at the guitar and the sound of Marta's high heeled shoes shuffling on my wooden floorboards and the barking of my voice, and in the end my stifled shout gave way to the guitar in the outro and then there was just the throb of the party in the walls again.

"I love it," Marta said and I croaked "thank you" and she smiled watery-eyed at me and said gently, suddenly fingering my collar, "but you need a band." And then she kissed me lightly on the lips and I only jumped slightly, and she shimmied closer to me on the bed and as I felt my cock harden there was the sound of breaking glass and a muffled shout from somewhere. Marta said "what the fuck," released me and started with speed to the door and I followed her to the kitchen where we found Rip grappling with some guy on the floor.

He had the guy pinned on his back, and was slamming a closed fist into the side of his head. I stared, then laughed at the crazy scene. There was a fresh, dark stain on the wall, and bright shards of green glass were scattered all over the floor. The pinned guy, a white, blonde-haired boy, squealed and struggled to get free but before he could find purchase on the floor and fight back, Marta and I rushed to Rip's aid. Marta punted the kid in the head with her high-heeled shoe, without hesitation, and I grabbed his legs and jostled Rip to one side of me so the three of us could pick the guy up and throw him out. He pitched and seized and seethed while we jerkingly walked him down the hall like we were taking him to a padded cell, and then someone scrabbled for the latch to the front door and we literally threw him through it, and he hit the garden path with a smack and then picked himself up and ran away, right away. He didn't look back and we didn't watch him go. Gently I shut the door on the night.

"What the fuck happened?" I said into the now-hushed hall as the three of us stood breathing hard in unison, and the rest of the party stood staring around us. Adrenaline reverbed through me like the echo of bashed sheet metal.

"Doesn't matter," said Rip, panting, slowly cooling, and he gulped and caught his breath. Then he said "bad party etiquette," with a shaky laugh, and folded his arms. "He won't do it again."

Everyone watched as Rip, Marta and I silently swept up the glass from the floor and did our best about the mess on the wall. A few people I didn't know asked if I was OK, and one guy wearing Birkenstocks said it was a bit much, throwing him out, but then I looked at him and he didn't say anything else. Then everyone else started to leave. It was late and people had stopped bothering to play music.

I was tired and too-wired, and not liking the slow onset of the coke's after-effects. The bourbon from under my bed appeared in my hand, and it was jammed in my mouth like a force-feeding funnel and I gulped and gulped, and when it came away from my lips I felt its pleasing warmth spreading through my limbs, like ink colouring water, and I smiled as my eyes dimmed. I leaned on a wall in the hall as the last few people either hung out in the doorway of Rip's room, or in the kitchen.

The bottle kept tilting up to my lips and just before I blacked out I saw Rip sat some place high up, surrounded by friends and wreathed in cigarette smoke, really laughing.

6.

The New Year had come and gone and then the winter after it, and it was 2011, and now it was light until the evenings, and I felt light. I was getting used to the house I lived in, relishing being free of family. I had discovered getting behind on bills. I met Rip's friends and they were there all the time and we talked about music, and the scene, and I worked out what the scene was and went to shows. I'd stuck it out at the coffee place so far, and Rip had just recently got a job at some office. We bitched about our work, but everything was OK.

Marta had got in touch with me in mid-January to offer me studio time: one of her friends ran a place and they had agreed, with Marta's leverage, to record me for cheap with a band who Marta said she would assemble. I'd felt a happy sick swoop sensation in my stomach when I got off the phone to her that day, and alone in my bedroom I punched the air and hissed "yessss." This would definitely lead to a real record coming out, I thought, and inevitable success soon after. I imagined myself being conveyed towards something nameless and brilliant and big, and on my way towards triumph I would process past everyone I'd ever known, who would clap and smile, realising that of course, of all the people they had met, the one to make it, and deservedly, would be me. After the phone call I strode around the living room while Rip read, and I rapturously said most of that to him, and he looked over the top of his book at me and said "mmhm."

Anyway I was glad Marta liked me, and "Freezin Rain", and hadn't been put off me by the awkwardness of our interrupted kiss. Passingly I wondered if she had told Rip. She told me to demo the song and send it to her, and then she'd send it to her friend. I recorded it standing at one end of my bedroom while my MacBook stood on my chest of drawers with the Voice Memos app running, and I cack-handedly bashed out the song, and emailed the crackling, out-of-tune result to Marta and she wrote back quickly, saying "*wow, lo-fi, love itt xxx*" and sent me a bunch of dates to choose from, and suddenly I was all set.

•

I winced when Sean clapped me on the back as he introduced me to his uni friends. I was shown into the hall of his parents' mansion, and instructed to take my shoes off as ten or so of his chums, some ruddy-cheeked, salmon-trousered lads, stuck their heads round a door to peer at me. They said guffawing hellos in drawls and one said "ah the rock and roll star" and Sean laughed and they all laughed, and Sean said "no no, ha, ha," and I said nothing and smiled dumbly and shuffled in my socks through to where the big birthday gathering was happening in a very high-ceilinged room, furnished with unsat-on sofas and actual chandeliers. There was a low pulse of chart music and the clink of fluted glasses. I told myself the next little while was going to be OK, but at the same moment noticed that my socked feet were leaving sweaty footprints on the hallway's flagstone floor.

Despite his lineage, Sean wasn't too bad. Only rich. He shoved a can of beer into my hand as he introduced me to his friends by saying "our mums used to be pals back in the day when they were both regular churchgoers," which earned a scoff from a few of the Hooray Henrys clamouring around him (there were no girls present), and I looked around the room distractedly, desperately. I quickly finished the beer, instantly itching for another, and another appeared, and I finished that too.

No one talked to me for the rest of the party. I had decided to leave at midnight, and then a fat man in a tie came up to me and slurred into my ear that they'd heard I was going to be a famous musician one day and then had his arm tight around my shoulder and was pouring tequila into my mouth and it went down my throat and he screamed with laughter, and he wouldn't take his arm from around me, and he kept on laughing and laughing.

I shut my eyes at the noise and then when I opened them he was gone and I was standing alone in the crowded room. Why am I such a cunt, I thought to myself and then I was sitting down. The pattern on the deep-pile rug beneath my feet was bungeeing in and out of focus. Fucking cunt, I thought.

I woke up to searing uncurtained daylight in one of the house's many rooms, not having made it home or undressing before collapsing onto the chintzy divan I was now peeling myself off of. I stink, I thought. Why am I such a cunt.

7.

I made myself get up and go downstairs despite the vice-like hangover helmet which encased my skull. On the landing I passed sprawling piles of Sean's friends, who seemed to have collapsed where they had been stood the night before but undressed, still and pink and glistening in morning sunlight, like just-discarded cuts of meat. I descended over gravel to the road, which led me to the train station, and I took a train back to London.

The Essex countryside passed me by, and I peered out of the carriage window as I was being borne back into the city. I passively watched as grey greens became greys, and there was more graffiti and more posters stuck to stuff and at Ilford there were more people piling into the carriage that I was on, and I spent the last twenty minutes of the ride with some guy's crotch in my face. He was wearing blue jeans and the button above his flies was imprinted with the words *M&S Collection* and the button was inviting somehow, and I thought about taking the top row of my teeth and applying them like a bottle opener to his trousers. I didn't want to look up to see the man's face. I thought about my parents' divorce.

Number Three was my contact at the old house, hanging back behind enemy lines, providing me with info on Mum and Dad's comings and doings, and had been the one to keep me informed about the glacial collapse of their marriage. She had called me to give me the news, and it was the first time I'd heard her voice since I'd left Brentwood, for what I'd thought then would be the last time. There was a new guy involved, I learned, and she'd gone somewhere hilarious like Braintree to live with him, and he was a cunt and Three had last seen Mum being picked up by him in an Audi TT.

"Is she going out with a gay hairdresser?" I asked. Three didn't laugh, rightly. That joke was out of date, even then.

"He's an electrician or something," she said, softly.

"Bizarre," I said. "How are you, anyway?" I asked, just as my phone ran out of battery. "Hello?" I said into the dead contraption, not realising.

8.

"I'm sorry I'm late," I said, wheezing as a heavy old door was unlocked and I was silently shown by a stranger into a dark corridor.

The forbidding building had been a barn and was now a studio, and I had come there to record "Freezin Rain". The place was flung out in the far reaches of North London, and I had got lost three times during my two hour journey there: once by taking the Tube in the wrong direction, then by getting the wrong bus and, finally, by walking past the place twice because it was sat back from the road with no sign, and I'd had no idea what kind of a joint I was looking for. It was the first hot day of the year and my shirt stuck to my skin and the guy showing me in touched my back as I came through the door, and he must have felt that it was cold with sweat. The ceilings in the place were low and we walked down the gloomy hall into a halogen-lit kitchen and he drew me up a chair and told me to wait there: Jim was just finishing setting something up, and would be with me shortly.

Jim Benson was the guy who owned Flower Gardener, the studio, the guy Marta had set me up with. He'd produced several records I liked and a ton more which were apparently famous but that I'd never heard of, and was, according to Marta, doing her and me a massive favour by agreeing to record me. I had one day to get my song right, and it was going to cost me two hundred quid, which had taken me about three months to save.

I heard footsteps scuffing down the long corridor which led from the kitchen to, I guessed, the studio itself, and then Jim Benson entered. He was older than me and had curly hair down to his shoulders, and wore a brown coat that he probably thought made him look like a lab technician, but which I thought made him look like a porter. He was white and he had a fat, handsome face. He smiled at me and shook my hand, and complimented me on the demo but his smile didn't reach his eyes and I wondered if he was lying.

"Welcome," he said and I said thank you, then wrinkled my nose, wondering why I'd said that, but he seemed not to be listening and told me to follow him down the corridor and he showed me the studio, the first I'd ever seen or been into.

There was a control room with a big electronic desk covered in mysterious sliders and buttons and knobs and some lights flashed on it, and above that and Jim's desk was a pane of glass which gave me a view into another, darkened room, where I guessed I would go to record my tune. Three figures skulked in the half light of that room, moving equipment around and twisting attachments onto long black poles and standing things up and folding things away, and Jim pointed them out to me as Andy (he was the guy who'd let me in), Tim, and Paul. They had a kind of humourless, homunculoid look about them, and were all thickset and about the same height and age as one another, and all wore shorts with chains dangling from them which jingled as they moved, inching carefully past the equipment in the small room which was piled high against its padded walls.

"So what we'll do," Jim said, too loud, placing a hand on my shoulder which he removed when I flinched, "is get your guitar down and do a scratch vocal on top of that" – I didn't say I didn't know what a scratch vocal was – "and then do a real vocal take and any overdubs after that. Listening to the demo," he went on – after I had tried to sound confident by saying "cool, cool" – "I think it'd be good to have a bass track on there, and Marta asked me about laying down some drums which I'm of course happy to do." I was flushed by the realisation that I was going to be going away with a full version of my song and not just a demo, done with nice mikes. It was what I had dreamed that I would do in a studio if I ever got to be in one, and now I was in one. I tried not to make my smile so big.

After the three studio dudes had finished setting things up, which took nearly an hour and a half which made me nervous because I was worried we'd run out of time and I'd have to pledge money I hadn't got to get the track finished, I was taken into the live room and sat with my guitar, getting miked up.

Jim came in to make sure everything was in its right place and saw me cradling my battered old acoustic, which I'd dragged with me from home. "Is that what you're going to be using for this?" he asked, and I told him yes. "Rrrright, OK. Well, we've got a lot of other guitars you could try," he waved vaguely at the room where there were indeed a shitload of expensive looking guitars lying around, "so maybe do a guide with that, um, that one, and then, uh, yeah. Yeah, let's give it a go. Stick your cans on and I'll have talkback in the room, so I can tell you when we're ready to go for one."

"My..?" I said. Jim stared at me blankly for a second.

"Headphones," he said, realising, catching himself, and then he bustled out of the room and Andy followed him, and I heard Andy quietly snort when I didn't know the proper term for headphones. I also don't know what talkback means either, if you want to take the piss out of that as well, you cunt, I thought. I put on my cans.

"OK, let's go for one," a tiny voice said in my ears, and I started to play right away and then the voice said "no, stop." I stopped. "I'm going to give you four. Wait for the clicks, OK?"

"The..?"

"The click track," said the voice. In the window to the other room I could only see the reflection of my own startled face. "OK," sighed the crackling voice, "there's going to be a count of four, that's the click, and after that you start playing, OK?"

"OK."

"OK? Here we go." The clicks clicked, and I tried to play. Jim had to tell me not to sing at the same time as playing the guitar – I didn't know about things being separately recorded – but eventually I did it.

"OK. I think we've got that down now," Jim said to me, finally, through the talkback, which I worked out was when he was the voice in my cans, from the control room. On the other side of the glass a light flicked on and I saw that Jim was the only person left in the room. "So let's do some drums now, to go with the guide, and then everything else proper." I said OK and Jim burst into the room without further warning and sat at the drums and put on his own pair of headphones and began pounding at the drum kit before I could get out, so I froze so as not to make a sound and just watched. He stopped after the duration of the song and said "alright, that should do it" and ushered me into the control room to listen to what he'd played.

I listened.

"That's good," I said. It was. Jim had done something loose but in time, simple but sharp and he understood it, and it was like The Fall or something, and I felt my whole self smile. I had made something, and it was coming into being.

"More guitar?" said Jim, and I said OK. "In here this time, with me." And I did it to his drums and it was good. "Vocals?" Jim said.

We stayed in the control room to do that, too. A microphone got set up by one of the homunculoids who had shufflingly turned back up, and I licked my lips as the track kicked in and then did my shout-singing thing. I hollered it out in one go, and there were no thoughts in my head and I didn't have to go back to the start. Jim's hand hovered over the desk when I was done and he turned and looked at me over his shoulder, and his eyes were still. He said "OK," which was how he started every sentence, but he was speaking softly now. "That was great. Let's do another one, for safety?" It was about three o' clock in the afternoon. I said sure and did another one all the way through, and Jim said OK again and there was a ringing silence in the sound-dampened control room. Andy, who was behind me, shuffled his feet. I turned to look at him and his face was impassive except he kind of raised his eyebrows at me. I remember feeling proud of impressing him, even if he was a stupid old fucker who'd been rude to me. Then Jim deemed my vocals done and I flinched as he slapped the sound desk with both palms and bellowed "bass!"

Then we were finished. The track was bounced down (which was like the music word for printing, or something), and polished and everything, and a copy was sent to my email address, and then I had to go. Everybody was standing in the kitchen and I had my back to the door, and motes of dust sauntered in the light cast by the naked bulb dangling from the ceiling. Jim had asked if I wanted him to send the song to Marta and I'd said "not yet." I thanked him for recording me, and did the I-don't-know-you smile and everyone did it back at me. Andy looked down at the ground as he did it.

"My pleasure," Jim said, suddenly doing that very professional smile again. We shook hands. "So did you want to pay today, or..?" I was making to leave as he said it, and everyone laughed as I stopped, and struggled to get my wallet out of my pocket.

9.

I did up the strings on my apron and placed two hands on the shop counter, drawing in a deep breath through my nose and releasing it through my mouth. I glanced down, as I did every morning, at the little piece of paper Euan had stuck to the till which read "Shoulders Down", and I put my shoulders down. Relax, I thought, as I often thought. It was six forty-five in the morning and orange sunshine glinted off the shopfront's steel and glass, and the daylight was magnified by the window, and warmed my face.

Sarah was unlocking the shop doors and showing in the people waiting outside, who had been queueing there for about ten minutes. They came in from the cold to order overpriced coffee served by me, half-conscious and with my hair sculpted by sleep into a weird conical hat.

That morning my mouth had the stale wet sock taste of last night's can of lager times ten, and I hadn't eaten since yesterday afternoon so I had bad shakes. I'd sneak a croissant later, I thought, when Sarah wasn't looking. She was OK but would grass me up without thinking about it if Bea asked her why something was missing. Bea was the manager, and mostly spent her time in the office looking at us via the CCTV display anyway, and so didn't need us to tell tales on one another. She once stormed out to the shop front to catch me with my mouth full of pastry, and called me a thief in front of colleagues and customers. I think the sweets cost Bean There about ten pence each; we were selling them for at least two quid a go.

A woman came up to the counter and ordered from me, and I made her order. She smiled at me and went away and the door tinkled as it shut behind her. I ran my tongue over my teeth. Then a man came up and placed his order, and I set about making his double macchiato. I gave it to him, and he suspended his wallet in mid-air and said "can I ask you a question?" I said sure and his face darkened and he jerked his head backwards at the just-closed door, and said "was that a man?" I stared at him blankly, knowing with a crushing feeling in my chest what he was getting at, but tried to pretend not to understand.

"Excuse me?" I said.

"You know, that person you just served, was that a man?" He had an American accent. It was early, still.

"I don't know," I said, very slowly with my eyes half open, and I tilted my head back and kept looking at him right in the face. "And I think... it's not very polite to ask." Then to my amazement he went on.

"Yeah but, like, is that a thing that's common here, in London?" I kept looking at him in the way that I was, and then he tried to be friendly, and chuckled and said, "I'm just visiting, I was just–"

"I don't know, and I really, really don't care," I said, sharply, and finally he shut his mouth. He paid for his coffee in sullen silence and when he got to the door he looked over his shoulder and said to me, "freak," and then he was gone. I waited til the last person in the waiting queue had got what they wanted and got out, and then I turned and punched the burnished metal of the espresso machine, hard, denting it and leaving a searing red graze on my knuckles. I looked and there was a smear of blood where my fist had been. Sarah said "what happened," and I said nothing, and I heard Bea's footsteps approaching from the back room.

•

I was spending June trying to get a gig. I called up venues to be told that they didn't do their own booking, and sent "Freezin Rain" to the promoters they put me on to, who told me they didn't book people they'd never heard of. I had felt flushed at my first rush of yeses, and so was then despondent at this sudden slew of nos. But then, I thought, if I asked a band that people had heard of to play a night I was putting together myself, I could stick myself on the bill and people would come and see it, and then they'd see me. I told Rip my idea and he recommended a group called EIO, so I messaged them and offered them fifty quid (not knowing where I'd get the money), and asked another band called Micron 53 if they would be up for it too, for less money (which I also didn't have), and everybody was saying yes again very quickly and I was very happy, because suddenly there was a lineup in which I was going to appear.

I was making myself play every day, in my room, ignoring the sick swoops of fear in my stomach whenever I thought about standing up in front of a group of strangers – and Rip – and singing a bunch of songs I had written myself. Rip's teasing about what he called my debutante's ball did not help me. I tried to ignore his "woo"s and "yeah baby"s through the wall as I rehearsed and rehearsed each new, inexpert song.

I decided I wanted the George Tavern for my show – it seemed fitting to play at my Damascene scene. Maybe Astrid, God's light, would turn up again too. At home after work one afternoon I called up the pub to reserve a date. I spoke to Helen on the phone, who began quizzing me about how many people would come and how much I'd be charging, and what kind of night was it anyway, and so I thought fast and said I'd be postering in the area, and people would come to see EIO after their successful headline show there last year, and they'd include the date on their tour posters, which would, like, definitely pull people in. (I didn't mention that the band *would* be on tour, but after my show was meant to take place, and in Europe.)

I would be playing first on the night, but billing myself as main support. I thought that people would see the poster and think I was a name they should have heard and so give me the time of day; and when they twigged that I was first on, maybe they'd think that the reason I'd been billed near the top but was playing early meant that I was some sort of surprise, a super-secret famous act who they definitely should have heard of. I thought it was a good wheeze and when I told Rip about it he looked up from his book, which he'd been using as a prop to ignore me, grinned, and went "ha!"

Rip said I had to have a name for my "club night" and so I chose Construction House, a stupid name that sounded good and that was just a literal translation of Bauhaus, whose "Terror Couple Kill Colonel" seven-inch I'd had on my turntable continuously since picking it up for cheap a few weeks previously. For the poster's artwork I printed out a picture I found online of a bespectacled Chinese kid, and then wrote the gig info over it in black marker, and Rip scanned me 50 copies on his work printer and there it was, and I put it up everywhere, and it was really happening, there was no backing out now. It was a little mantra I repeated to myself, no backing out now, the words of some kind of half-encouraging stiff-upper-lip-type dad, the kind I hadn't had.

Construction House presents: EIO, w/ Jude &
Micron 53. George Tavern, August 28th, 8PM, Four Quid

All in my scrawl over a picture of a Chinese kid. I couldn't think of a suitable stage name so I just used my Christian name, or my Jew name, as Rip called it. I thought that was funny. I remember retorting with some Chinese joke, probably because of the poster, and he didn't punch me like he usually did when I cracked wise at his expense, only looked away and said "fuck off" under his breath.

•

EIO were setting up their gear in the centre of the George Tavern floor. In my head an all pervasive "A" rang through the air as I imagined them as an orchestra, in a pit, tuning up while I, an actor, breathed deeply behind a velvet curtain, and made final adjustments to my costume before appearing onstage.

In fact I was sitting at the bar peeking nervously over the rim of a pint glass, beer busily foaming in my throat, and at the bottom of my otherwise empty stomach. I'd just about been able to go over to the group and say hello earlier and now I was openly fiddling with an envelope that contained their fee – I didn't understand I was supposed to take it out of the door money, or know about setting up a float or anything. Helen had said she'd come and help me with some things when I arrived but she had disappeared, and now I was everyone's go-to guy and I willed no one to speak to me until she returned, or at least until Rip showed up. He said he was coming straight after work but I knew he'd go home first, and he was always late for everything.

It was six forty-five and the breezy sound of late-summer cars washed around the bar, and the street had dimmed from the day's bright harsh yellow into a low purple-and-gold glow, which leaned softly in through the open door.

EIO were two women guitarists, and two men who played drums and bass. I thought I remembered talking to the lead singer at some show, but the memory was in slow-mo, and you know that look of concern you get from people when you're shitfaced and jack-in-the-boxing back and forward, and trying to make sense but probably scaring them? I thought maybe I did that to her, and that night was just a beige blur, and probably she didn't remember me, but being embarrassed by my stupid drunk behaviour made me too shy to find out.

My second pint loosened me up. I slid off my barstool and shuffled over to the band who looked as if they were ready to go for a run through of a song, and I said hello. They said hi back in unison. Rachel and Billie were the singers, respectively black and white, short and tall, older than me; the bass player and drummer were called Oggy and Matt: one tall one short, both white, also older, but acted younger. I mentioned Rip recommending them to me as headliners, and Matt looked up at me as I looked down at his sandalled feet and in a flash I recognised him: he was the guy who had mouthed off about the kid we threw out at the party. He had maintained and even seemed to have somewhat cultivated his mean and shifty air since I'd last seen him. Up close now, and soberish, I realised his grubby appearance didn't just come from the overalls which he wore half-on and tied at the waist, but that he was dirty and I could smell him at five paces, and he had those same Birkenstocks on, and some stupid obscure band T shirt. Oggy was a plummy-voiced, long-haired long streak of piss, with big teeth. I later learned the two of them had gone to a posh school together, a fact belied by their matching bohemian poses, and identikit cool-guy haircuts.

The sound guy who came with the place gave the band the OK, and EIO eased through a song of theirs, "Running Room," a coolly cantering number that featured Rachel and Billie's calls and responses over jagged and sparse guitars, over Matt and Oggy's lolloping, sunny rhythm section. Matt sped up throughout the song and before they started he asked "how does this one go again?" But together the rumbling ensemble was charismatic, and they smiled when they played. I stopped worrying about not having an audience, and started to worry about having one.

EIO cleared off and it was my turn to check. I strapped on my guitar and bashed out a couple of chords and cleared my throat, and the sound man who was one of those big-haired kids from before asked me if that was the guitar I was going to use, and sighed when I said yes, and told me that he'd have to find his contact mike. "You should get an electric," he said over his shoulder, up to his elbows in black wire, irritated, as he hunted out a means of amping up my guitar. It's my night, I wanted to say, but didn't. He asked me if I wanted any effects and I asked for some slapback, and he let me get through half a song before stopping me, saying the other band needed to get on. They'd just walked through the door, late, and started setting up their gear around me before I got offstage.

Eight thirty came, and I was soon due to play. Helen appeared and started hassling me about people's IDs and other things that I didn't know how to manage (she kept on telling me things were my responsibility "as the promoter") and making me regret having done this at all and I was scared of her, and all

I could think about was having to step up onstage in front of the twenty or so people who had already dutifully filed in to watch the show. I thought I recognised some faces from the party, and wondered if Rip had made sure people turned up to watch me. He hadn't turned up yet.

Eight forty-five came and I couldn't put off playing any longer, and so the room drew me into its centre and my black old beaten guitar winked at me as I came to a stop in front of it. I picked it up and turned on the spot to face the microphone, and there was feedback as it came up and the lights went down. I drew in a breath and there was the sound of a car whipping by outside, and then I began to play.

"*You softly said as I climbed the stairs to bed/'I would like to be cremated when I die'*" I sang in the cold-opening verse of "Glacial Goodbyes" over clunking and mournful chords. As I sang, something happened. A few people looked over at me from the bar, and then everybody did, and by the song's first soft chorus I wasn't scared and I was feeling good, and the rest of my show melted into shapeless softness, supple, and under my smiling control. The song finished. There was light applause which sounded like far-off rain, and my ears rang. I paused for too long and someone whistled.

"Thanks," I croaked into the mike. Then I played "Freezin Rain" for the next one, and during that number I felt a feeling which I would come to love, a little switch that flicked that was everyone in the room listening only to me, their attention one. I could hear people listening to my words, and I dreamed I heard the intake of breath of one girl at the song's opening line, a gasp following the word "fist." They clapped that song too, and each one until I finished, and when I came offstage to more non-sarcastic-sounding applause a guy I didn't know came up to me and said "I'd never have the balls to do that," like it was a good thing I'd done. It hadn't occurred to me to do it any other way.

Rip materialised from the thinning crowd to slap me on the back and steer me to the bar, and told me that he'd only just arrived in time because he didn't want to put me off, but I knew he was embarrassed to be too encouraging before my first ever show. "Baby's first gig" he kept calling it.

10.

Bean There closed for the week between Christmas and New Year because the owner had gone on holiday with his family, and so Sarah, Euan and I lost out on shifts and money while Bea got paid a Christmas bonus for "great leadership" and hitting some sales target. She printed off and showed us the congratulatory email sent to her by the owner. I had visions of stuffing it down her throat. I think she was about twenty-five. I wondered about people, sometimes.

To cover myself until we opened back up, I'd taken a job house-sitting for this posh couple I'd met at work. They lived a street up from Rip and me, in one of the old naval houses on the Whitechapel Road. The building had once been used as a shop and so had a flat-roofed single storey jutting out from its front, and I was going to sit in the upstairs living room above it and make sure no one shimmied up the drainpipe to steal the lead tiles.

Howard was an architect, and doing the place up; Danuta worked for the BBC and I'd got talking to her one morning at work because I overheard her mention "the Ono interview" on the phone while I served her. After she hung up I asked her about it and at first her eyes flashed but then they softened when I flinched, and then she said that she was excited but nervous. I dared her to ask a Lennon question and she laughed and said that she'd try. I didn't see her for a few weeks after that but when she next came by, with Howard this time, I got the job. She and Howard were a young couple and they had a kid, a little girl.

Rip and I decided to have Christmas Day away from Essex in our flat, alone, with no family or other friends. I was glad to have him to myself. It felt like forever since we'd sat down and listened to our shared records together. We spent the day in his room, eating junk and opening the stupid joke presents we'd got each other. Neither of us knew how to cook, so we didn't try. I knew Christmas was over when I drunkenly put some fake mistletoe in my flies and tried to get Rip to kiss it. He punched me in the balls and I fell down laughing, and later passed out on the floor of his bedroom, waking up at three in the morning, unblanketed and freezing while he writhed above me in bed.

On Boxing Day Rip took a cab his parents had booked him back to their place in Brentwood, and I moved into the naval house for the week. All I had to do was make it look like someone was home in the evenings, leave lights on, things like that, and I also had to feed Howard and Danuta's two mangy cats twice a day. The place was freezing in its old age and uncentrally heated, so I kept to the upstairs living room and delighted in lighting a fire and huddling in front of it, feeding the flames with logs from the woodpile on the hearth.

Their telly had Sky, and in the evenings I sat reading with the news channel droning in the background, all lights on, luxuriantly wasting electricity. It was probably good to be making noise to deter any stalking lead thieves, anyway, I thought. I imagined myself as a night watchman, hooded and hunched with a lantern and shouting "who goes there" at the first scrape of a footstep. Of course no one tried anything, but I had tested the weight of a fire iron in my hand, in case.

Then it was the thirtieth of December. I'd taken to sleeping til two and staying up til past five, stretching my legs by prowling half-dressed through the house and chasing the cats around, and lightening the cupboards of any leftover non-perishables.

I was supine on the sofa with my legs crossed at the ankles, the copy of *Heavier Than Heaven* I was half-reading dangling from my hand. The fire crackled and I could feel my eyes drifting closed when my phone buzzed in my pocket. I shook myself, took it out and looked to see a text from Astrid, which read "*Yr on the list Jude, come to box office early doors 2 get yr pass.*" I yelled "yes!" and punched the air, and the cat that had been sitting by my feet leapt up and hissed as it ran from the room.

The list Astrid was talking about was Springs Eternal's New Year show at Hammersmith Apollo, the group's first London gig in years, and the ticket everyone was trying to get a hold of. The Rayographs' label had lucked out and been able to get the band booked as openers on the bill, so Astrid had some guest list to dole out. I'd got in touch with her in September to try and book her group for a show of mine (which never happened), but it was what started an ongoing (sometimes one-sided) conversation that led to me getting her number, and persistently and unashamedly pestering her to get me into that gig. When she'd politely declined the invitation to play my show she'd enigmatically asked me if I had got any tunes together yet, I said yes and she'd asked to hear, so I sent "Freezin Rain" as recorded by Jim Benson and she said she liked it. I didn't hear anything more about the track, but now she was inviting me to a fucking Springs Eternal gig, on New Year's fucking Eve.

Springs had formed in the '80s and been going ever since, and had changed the entire conversation around modern guitar music, and you could still go into any venue anywhere and see some young group ripping off their schtick. Young dudes still copied singer-guitarist Harrison Dalby's haircut, that he'd sported since twenty years ago, a mop-top with fringe way over the eyes, and even now that he was in his fifties he was still considered achingly hip and people would fawn over him like he was the biggest, coolest thing ever, which to me and people like me he totally was. I went to bed that night shivering with excitement for the day that was to come.

Rip called me in the morning. He asked me about our plans for the night and my insides groaned as I remembered that I said we'd sit up for the countdown to midnight in the naval house, since neither of us had made any other plans, and he'd got back to London a day earlier than he thought.

"I'm not going to be in after all," I said, with trepidation.

"What? No I know, you're house sitting still, right? I thought we were going to hang out there." His voice echoed, and I could hear the little sticking sounds his bare feet made as he padded around our empty flat.

"No, I– Astrid invited me to the, um, the New Year's show," I said, my stomach curling hotly in at its edges.

"Astrid?" said Rip, and I realised I hadn't mentioned that she and I had even talked past the first time we'd met. There was a beat with crackling breath and then Rip said, "what New Year's show?"

"Springs Eternal," I said, spitting the words out like seeds, or flies.

"That's been been sold out for–"

"Yeah I know," I said, "she only told me last thing last night, otherwise I would've–"

"Yeah, yeah. No, Yeah." The phone line thrummed. Rip waited, and my words pressed into the painful silence.

"To be honest I don't know if it's for me, or for me and a plus one, so..." My eyes widened in surprise as my mouth gave shape to the first lie that came into my head.

"What do you mean?" Rip said, sounding suddenly bored and annoyed.

"Uh, I just mean... Well, Astrid just said that my tickets were on the door, so–"

"Tickets plural?"

"Maybe, I don't know," I said, mouth clacking, dry.

"Why don't you come down to the venue with me, I'll be going early to see the Rayographs' set anyway, and then we can try the ticket trick?"

"Hmm."

The ticket trick was when you went in past venue security with your pass, then met up with someone else who you knew who was already inside, borrowed their pass, came back out and gave it to your passless friend, and then you both walked back through security together. Presto, the ticket trick.

"Alright, why not," Rip said, and then the line crackled as he sighed through his nose. "What time are you going down?"

•

I was pretty drunk by the time Rip and I got on the Tube at Stepney Green. As our train rattled westward, I swung around a pole and Rip told me to shut up when I started to sing a few bars of a Springs Eternal song. I stood up for most of the journey and he sat in his seat looking at his phone, legs crossed tightly at the knee and his right foot jigging up and down. I'd been self-conscious about what to wear and had pestered Rip about it endlessly when he arrived and wore him down til he told me "black, always black" and it wasn't until we were too far away from the naval house that I realised there was a god damn deodorant mark all down the front of my button-up shirt, and I resolved to wash it off in the bathroom when we arrived, but forgot. I would shortly be too pissed to care. Nobody would notice, probably. I remember some other anxiety about UV lights but I think it was short-lived. Sighing sound as I opened another can and sour lager chugged down my throat and then sat down next to Rip and belched in his ear. He laughed in spite of his bad nervous mood. Fellow gig-goers got on our carriage as we passed through town, wearing Springs Eternal shirts which was very lame, one wearing a Pop Group tee, though, which was quite cool, and Rip began to perk up somewhere around Royal Oak. I burped again and a few heads turned and one girl said "ugh," and I laughed.

We pulled into Hammersmith and a flood of people exited the station and marched with hushed excited voices like pilgrims going up to a shrine, and Rip and I walked with them under the overpass and I vibrated as I came up to the gigantic gleaming doors of the Apollo.

"Wait here for me," I said to Rip, "I'll go to the box office and get mine, and then let you know where to go." He nodded his assent while chewing on a fingernail and I flashed him a wonky smile as I turned and pulled the push door, and then pushed it with a laugh and shoved my way inside.

I asked the one inattentive security guy standing in the lobby where to go if I was on the list and he eyed me up and down before pointing me to the box office, where there was no queue and I levitated in my smugness over the atrium's red deep pile carpet to the booth. I gave my name to the lady behind the glass, and her eyes flicked upwards once to my face and then she handed me a little envelope which contained a green sticker which read: *RFM Concerts presents SPRINGS ETERNAL* and then under that there was a blank space in which was written *"AAA"* and in that moment I could have puked from the adrenaline that was ballooning in my chest.

One pass, though, not two. But I knew that: in half-convincing Rip that he might get in (and that I might try to get him in), I'd kind of convinced myself too. I thought of him hopping from foot to foot in the cold outside. I stepped to one side of the ticket booth, leaned against a pillar and, running my thumb over the emboss of the triple-A pass, pulled my phone out of my pocket and dialled. He answered on the second ring.

"Any joy?" he said, a slight tremor in his voice. I paused and he said "hello?"

"Hi," I said, "Listen I'm really sorry–"

"No, it's–"

"I asked the lady at the box office if there was any chance of a spare and she said the list is totally full, and security look like they're pretty on it... I don't really know what to–"

"It's fine," Rip said flatly. "You tried."

"Well... what will you do now?" I said, strange relief mixing with the guilt gnawing at my gut.

"I don't know," Rip said, "probably see if any of my uni mates are home yet, hang out with them."

"I'm sorry–"

"Stop apologising, dude," Rip said, cutting me off. "It's fine, you asked and they said no, I'll go to a party somewhere, you have a good night."

"I know, but I'd much rather you were here," I said, surprised by my reflexive answer's untruth.

"We don't have to spend *all* our time together," he said, irritably, fast. "Don't worry about it, get me Dalby's autograph or something, OK?"

"OK," I said, "Well, happy new year and, uh, I'll see you next year!" I said it too loud and Rip didn't laugh and he quickly said "OK bye" before hanging up.

I peeled the back off my pass and stuck it to the inside of my jacket, and I flashed it at the bored security guy who half-looked at it as he showed me through the door to the live room, and I made my way in and down a slope towards a huge stage, lit from the bottom in white and draped in black velvet.

11.

A cheer went up from the small crowd who were already encamped at the barrier in preparation for the main event, and I saw Astrid leading the four other spot-lit Rayographs out onto the stage, and their shadows were cast big across towering black drapes, making them look like stalking hyenas, and their hair was black and wild. Astrid was walking tall, and grandly strapped on her Orpheus guitar in one sweeping flourish, seeming bigger and brighter than I'd seen her before. Her teeth flashed and she softly said "hello" into the microphone, which glittered. Barely giving the rest of the group time to plug in and position themselves behind their instruments, she hollered a count of four and they rumbled into life. Their music had a low and threatening feel that Astrid on her own hadn't had, but her voice rang clear through the murk and her bandmates were camouflaged against the stage backdrop in comparison to her ferocity, and beauty.

I was mesmerised all over again. For twenty-something minutes that felt like seconds I was open-mouthed and forgot the jostling crowd around me; then I saw a light flash from the sound desk, the signal that the band had time for one last song, and so Astrid led her group though the strains of the final number she had played for the tiny crowd at the George, which I knew by now was called "Lighter To Bear" and I helplessly swayed as before, and then it came to a close. The group took a bow to criminally scattered applause, and then melted into the blackness of the wings as the house lights came up to illuminate the widening stream of pilgrims making their way down the slope.

I raced to the front of the hall and asked somebody about getting backstage, making a show of showing my pass, and was unceremoniously ushered through a side door and left standing alone in a chilly corridor, which was old and tiled and smelled of a swimming pool, and was painted avocado green. I made my way up a cold flight of stairs, one hand running along the wall as if mapping my progression through a labyrinth, and heard and followed the sound of chattering and clinking glass, and came upon the Rayographs' dressing room. They were towelling sweat off themselves and laughing and all looked up with catlike grins upon their faces as I knocked gently on the open door.

"You were really, really great," I said to the back of Astrid's head as she walked into the room ahead of me after inviting me in, and a bottle of beer appeared in my hand and she introduced me to the band. I thanked her in a cloth-mouthed voice for getting me on the list and she waved my thanks away, perching elegantly on the edge of a plastic chair with her back to the dressing room mirror. The room was small and hot, and I began to sweat. I easily chatted to her bandmates and realised how drunk I was as I drained my bottle, and made a note to slow down now, before I got too messed up.

The Rayographs were Astrid, Gabriel, Dom, and Nick, they were all white and very nice and I guess had been prepped on me by Astrid because they were clearly being effortfully nice, despite my drunkenness which was now obvious and I felt my lips curl into a leer and my neck craned in a weirdish way, and the room bent up at its edges in sympathy with my mouth and everybody's eyes got wider, and brighter, and I suddenly felt mean and full of a cruel laugh that I thought about letting out and just as I was going to whisper something close to Gabriel's ear, Astrid said at my elbow,

"Jude, have you got a sec?" I nodded sure and retreated with her to a corner where she said in suddenly hushed tones, "I've got a confession to make."

"Oh yeah?" I slurred.

"You know that demo you sent me?" Astrid asked. I

nodded. "Well, I should have checked with you before, so don't kill me, but I've just recently started up this label and we're looking–" a high pitched ringing sounded off in my ears and the murmur of the room receded to the far distance, "–for artists to contribute, and so I thought tonight might be a good time to talk a bit about it, and to meet Harrison who's–"

"Sorry," I said, suppressing a rising belch, "Harrison–?"

"Yeah sorry, Harrison Dalby," Astrid said, smiling. "We're working on this new label together, it's all really small fry, but between you and I that's how we got onto the bill, and kind of why you're here too." Dazed, I thought about how Rip would've corrected her "I" to "me" and I just stared at her, the ringing growing louder in my ears, and she hurriedly said "anyway, do you want to meet him? We've been looking for the right solo artist since we started and your stuff could be, well, what we've been looking for." I tried to say something, but only croaked, and then choked on a hunk of phlegm caught in my throat. The building rumbled around us and the tiny dressing room felt buried within it, like a seed. She was looking at me expectantly and from behind my fist as I coughed I nodded and managed to mouth "great" and she beamed, and then without a second's pause and while I was still spluttering she began dragging me by the arm into the corridor. I suddenly felt full of fear and too smashed and unsteady to meet Harrison and his band, but Astrid kept her hand in a firm grip on my upper left arm, and I was yanked into a jog in her wake, and we clattered down the green corridor together.

The door to the Springs Eternal's dressing room was unassuming, the presence of the group behind it only announced by a sheet of A4 paper blue-tacked to the door, but as it was opened after Astrid knocked and we walked in, I felt like I was passing through some kind of event horizon, and that I should expect to somehow fuse with this new glittering landscape. We walked into a huge and crowded room, filled with a sea of heads and hairdos, and people were openly smoking indoors. And there they were, the four of them, those names that I knew made flesh, leaning rigidly like rifles against the backs of hard backed-chairs. Dim light hid the slight cracks in the faces of the two women and two men, and festoons of food and drinks were piled high like offerings behind them on an altared table. I zoned in on Harrison Dalby at the end of the row of four, a guy whose image I had seen countless times on record sleeves, in videos, rock docs, posters above beds, posters on bar walls, posters in retro record shop windows, and looming in my mind's eye as I'd just been dragged down a corridor to meet him.

There he was, standing up now and animated in front of his crowd at six foot eight and beaming avuncularly at his admirers, seeming to conduct several conversations at once and with such easy ease, a crackling lightning rod for charisma. The room's scarce light seemed drawn to him, like it was reflecting off water and onto his face. He made eye contact with Astrid as she entered the room and waved at her, his eyes briefly meeting mine which made my stomach flip over, and she beamed back at him and guided me to the front of the throng, and a tall gin and tonic appeared in my hand as we made our way through.

"Hey," Astrid cooed at Dalby as we arrived.

"What's goin' on baby," he said in his pronounced New York drawl. The two of them embraced and as they came apart Astrid introduced me, saying, "this is the guy I told you about." This is fucking insane, I thought.

"Oh, right on," Dalby said, giving my hand a hard shake, and I mutely beamed and he continued, "I loved your song, man, it's ill." I squeaked out a thank you. "So, do you wanna?" Dalby said. I stared. "Make... a record... with us?" His eyes and smile widened as he spoke, kind and slow.

"Yes," I subvocalised, and Dalby laughed and said,

"alright, well let's meet in the New Year to talk about it, I'm asking some other people to come in and record too, so it'll be some time around then. We'll do you in February or something, cool?"

"We were thinking of using my studio, I live there at the moment actually," Astrid chipped in eagerly. "Does that sound good?" I said that it did, and laughed as we chinked glasses, and then then my anxiety and excitement and doubt and fear all disappeared, as did thoughts of Rip rattling back towards Stepney Green, and I sank in total ecstasy into the evening.

After Rayographs it was The Pop Group's turn to play, and Harrison said we should go and check them out. I drained my glass and followed. He and Astrid and I moved from the dressing room to the side of the stage, and watched the giant Mark Stewart writhing and screaming to the pummelling dub soundtrack of his band, and their light show was blinding and I looked out from under my hand's visor to the crowd which had grown to fill the cavernous concert hall, and who were standing in huge grin formation, fluorescing like glow-in-the-dark vampire teeth.

I lurched as the whole building tilted, and Harrison grabbed out for my shoulder, steadying me. The Pop Group were too intense and as Stewart howled like a wolf at the crescendo to "We Are All Prostitutes," I staggered backwards to a bathroom and dunked my head under life-giving water, then stared in a cracked mirror at my reflection and watched it change in front of me.

I came back to the wings, and Dalby and Astrid were gone. I sat down next to a girl who was sitting down too, watching the now-empty stage. We talked but I don't remember what about, she was older than me, and laughed at something I said.

I looked up as Liquid Liquid stepped over the girl's

and my head as she talked, and they stepped back again and I realised they'd played and finished their set without me noticing. There was a beat with a buzz in the air and then it was almost midnight, and as I sensed a presence behind me the girl stood and turned round to practically bow to Springs Eternal, who were there in single file and ready to go onstage: Harrison Dalby was in the lead of his troop, followed by Suzie, Luke, Robert, instruments in hand and emitting cool breeze and somebody ushered us out of their way, and they drifted serenely past us to take their places, and I watched with my heart almost joyously bursting as Harrison brought out with him a bottle of champagne which he sprayed onto the front row of the crowd as the clock struck twelve.

"Happy New Year," he said into his mike, centre stage, and it was 2012 as the opening discord of "God, With Long Legs" rang out, and I was swept forward on a wave of other hangers-on pushing at the side of the stage, getting as close as they dared to the band's burning intensity. Thrown forward by the breaking wave I lost my hold of the girl's hand, and met her eye for one last second as I had my sudden and brilliant idea: to run ahead of the surge, out to where Springs Eternal reigned like monolithic islands bursting from the sea, and dive over the edge of the stage.

I flew through pulsating air in which sweat droplets hung in suspended animation, turning warmly with my eyes closed and feeling the crowd's seaspray on my face, the apotheosis of the night's bliss. Then I opened my eyes and there was deafening noise and no one in the crowd caught me and I was winded as I slammed, hard, to the ground. People were shoving to get away from me; from where I was on the floor they disappeared like felling trees. Someone kicked me hard in the head.

Then loads of pairs of hands were upon me, dragging me roughly from the sticky theatre floor. I was wrenched through a spiky mangrove of elbows and knees and someone poured beer down the back of my neck, and then I was thrown into a corridor which was oppressively silent and black. A guy stormed out of the darkness and said "fucking stagediving, for fuck's sake, who the *fuck*–" and ripped my triple-A pass from the inside of my coat, and I was seized again by the strange hands and marched to a door, and then flew through the air again, but I watched myself flying this time, from somewhere up above.

Then I was back in my body and outside on the ground in the cold, and a fire exit door slammed shut behind me. I walked down the side alley of the Apollo, so drunk, and it was dark, and I could barely see but for the fireworks bursting miles above my head.

I staggered from the alley to the street. I got a text from Astrid as I sat astride a bollard, angling a line of spit from my mouth to the curb. She'd heard what had happened, and was coming to get me. She'd tell me later that to get me back in she'd had to pretend I was her brother, and not quite right in the head, and that she and I were both very very very very sorry. When she found me I was only bemused, too pissed to feel bad just then.

I was taken inside, and I remember being back in Springs Eternal's dressing room and not really registering that I'd missed the show I'd wanted to see so much, and my mouth tasted of burning gross acid and I wondered if I'd thrown up already. I shambled up to a sweat-drenched Dalby and burbled "can I have your autograph," and he looked at me like I was insane.

Then something happened, and I crashed backwards into Springs Eternal's rider table and knocked a whole bunch of bottles to the ground. I was hurriedly ushered out, by Astrid maybe, and then, she and her bandmates were packing their shit up around me and wearing coats and ready to go and it was four o' clock in the morning. I felt very lonely as I saw Astrid and Harrison kissing at the stage door. Then I was piled into a van and it rattled from Hammersmith to Seven Sisters, and I sucked on a bottle of John Smiths I'd lifted from somewhere. Gabriel was sitting opposite me in the van with his back towards the advancing road, and orange light flashed metronomically across his sleeping face, in time to the sigh of the motorway.

We arrived outside the Rayographs' studio and I fell out of the van as its sliding door whooshed open, and somebody roughly picked me up and leant me against cold brick. I leaned on my knees as I puked, and then I threw my pilfered bottle into the air and watched it go up and come down, and it smashed into pieces in the road. Gabriel turned to me and stage-whispered "what the fuck are you doing" but speech failed me and he left it alone, shaking his head and making his way up a clanging metal staircase to a door. I was led up the same stairs to the same door, and then the floor came up to greet me, and I went into oblivion as the sun began to rise.

•

I woke up to pale late afternoon light piercing my eyelids, and my phone buzzing against my skull. I peeled it off my face, looked at the screen which said Unknown Caller, and answered with a groan into the receiver. A small, high voice said,

"Um."

"What?" I said, hacking phlegm from my throat.

"Um," said the voice again, "Is this Jude?"

"Yeah, who's this?" They said a name I didn't hear. The connection was bad, and their voice kept cutting out.

"——Rip——they——d to go now——"

I screwed my eyes shut with the effort of piecing

together the broken infor-mation.

"——lo?"

I stood up with the phone clamped to my ear and the signal slightly improved, so then I clambered onto the back of a chair and I listened as a distant voice told me what had happened to Rip as he was heading home the night before.

PART TWO

12.

Harrison held open the pub door for me and I sidled past him, and I scanned the dim room for a place to sit as he came in behind me and clapped me on the back. He swaggered past me to the bar, saying over his shoulder, "what'll you have?" Meekly I asked for a Guinness.

"Two Guinness," Harrison said to the barmaid, who recognised him but didn't say so. The rest of the room did, too, the daytime drinkers looking everywhere but where we were. Some weren't bothering to be coy, though: a guy took out his phone and snapped a picture of us, and Harrison bared his teeth in a rictus grin as the unashamed flash went off. He and I then locked eyes for a second and he smirked, then turned back to pay for the beers, then handed one to me. I said thank you and followed him to a table by the window.

We smiled at each other as we bit into the biscuity heads of our pints. He swallowed, cleared his throat and said, "so." I smiled and said "so" too.

"Good to see ya, baby," he said.

"Good to see you," I said, "thanks for meeting me."

"Of course. So did Astrid tell you any more about the label?" I shook my head as I accepted another mouthful of beer.

"Not really," I said, swallowing.

"Well, it's small."

"Uh huh."

"And we're interested in having a kind of singles club vibe, you know, bespoke but kind of broad in range." He seductively drew out the word range, and took another slow sip of his pint. "Love your demo, by the way, we think it's a great song. We want cool stuff that's not only going to sell, but also review well, and we're confident about your, y'know, whole deal."

"Right," I said, keenly bobbing my head and smiling with politely pursed lips, images of my name in print passing before my eyes. "Because, yeah, what's the point otherwise." Harrison looked at me unblinking over the horned rims of his glasses, waiting. "Because, y'know, why put something out if no one hears it." My beer glass floated up to my lips, and more cool silk liquid passed over my teeth and down my throat. It felt good.

"Right," he said. He paused, suspending his glass in midair. He had the habit of leaving dramatic gaps between pronouncements, an interview technique I guessed, which always made me wonder if he was about to burst out laughing or fly into a rage, and so I closely followed every beat of his speech. "Right!" he said more again, more forcefully, and I jumped as he banged down his pint on the table.

"The money, and the effort, and, yeah," I said, looking down, suddenly aware of my heartbeat.

"The money is *right*," Harrison said, raising his eyebrows, half-laughing. "People assume I got money comin' outta my ass because of Springs royalties and whatever but, y'know, it's been a while since I've seen any of *that*."

"Really?" I said. I had also assumed Harrison was rich, since he was famous, and especially since he was able to spend money on putting out my record.

"You bet," he said, mid-gulp. Then he breathed out hard, and his eyes roved around the bar. "I mean, I can *get* other stuff, I'm lucky that I know enough people in London who can hook me up with shows, and I've done some voice over stuff– oh yeah," he said as I raised my eyebrows with interested disbelief, "some nature shit, it was real fun." He smiled to himself and said, "but hey, y'know, maybe I could work here. It's a short commute." I laughed and told him about working in a coffee shop, and that he really didn't want to get involved in the service industry if he could avoid it.

"Fair enough," he said, laughing too. We meditated on money and the things that were to come and then he said, "so you'll come in February, to Astrid's place?"

"Yes please," I grinned.

"Right on."

We stepped out into the darkening street and made to go our separate ways, him back up to a more salubrious end of Stoke Newington, me back east to Stepney, and a car pulled up beside us in traffic and the people in it recognised Harrison, and excitedly waved to him through the window as I stood like a proud pet at his heels. He smiled serenely and looked once at me before turning away, saying, "I guess they must be big Jude Hughes fans."

We said our goodbyes and I watched him as he sloped down the street, hands thrust into the pockets of his jeans. He turned a corner and was gone, and I turned around, and went home.

•

"OK, so for this one," Harrison said, "I want you to think about Arthur." I waited. "Uh... Think about Arthur, and, uh, what he meant to people. Think about his voice." I said OK and watched Harrison through the glass in the control room. He took his finger off the button and patted down his clothes distractedly, hunting for a lighter, a precariously dangling fag stuck to his lower lip. He was talking about Arthur Russell, whose music he'd shown me a few weeks ago, and was telling me to use him as inspiration for the take. I thought about telling Rip about it later, but then the knot that had been in my stomach since New Year's Day twisted tighter, and I tried to put him out of my mind.

"You're sounding great," Astrid said in a soft voice over talkback, leaning into my field of vision. She and Harrison were stood in the window in front of me, like people on TV, but who could talk to me. I shuffled my feet on the cold studio's thin carpet tiles, and rotated my shoulders. I was back in Seven Sisters, working on my record for the new label. The label didn't have a name yet, and Harrison kept on saying to me "you're on the ground floor, baby," when we talked about how it was all going. The studio was a warehouse conversion and freezing, and the floor was concrete and the Rayographs had tried to unindustrialise the space as much as they could with nice drapes and things, but it was still pretty bare. There was a fine layer of brick dust everywhere, and the arse on my black jeans had gone orange.

The Rayographs had been very pissed off about my embarrassing behaviour at the New Year's Eve show, but I gave everyone some space for about a week or so, and then went around apologising, playing up the part of the stupid little kid (which didn't take much effort), and everything seemed as though it was fine again. And here I was, back again.

"Freezin Rain" was in the can, and I was now losing my voice to "Glacial Goodbyes". Before the third take I took a deep, dusty breath.

"I think you're almost there, Jude," Astrid said.

•

It got dark and Harrison stopped the session, because it was late and he was hungry, and, he said, "Jude's about to pass out from the passion he's giving those vocals, man." He clapped me heartily on the back as I stepped out of the booth, and he said we'd finish the second song tomorrow, and then do overdubs, and then a monitor mix before the final mix, which would take place elsewhere. I nodded studiously at all of this, while feeling overwhelmed. Nobody said anything about what would happen after all that.

I grabbed my bag which contained two beers lifted from the studio fridge, and sat on the sofa in the common area and rolled a fag. There were ten minutes until the next bus came. Harrison came and sat down on the other sofa opposite me with an end of the day sound in his voice, like the disappearing sound of a car's engine. I could hear Astrid rattling around in the next room.

"Great one today, man," Harrison said. I said thank you, and bashfully looked down. He'd never mentioned the New Year's show to me and so, I thought, I wouldn't to him. I often think about how I could have fucked up the whole thing just hours after it being offered to me. If I had fucked it up I'd have probably remarked upon how that sort of thing was typical of me. It wasn't, really.

"So like, what's 'Freezin Rain' *about*," Harrison said suddenly. Everything he said sounded sarcastic in his Upstate articulation, but when I looked up at him he was smiling at me earnestly, kind of expectantly, like a kid.

"It's about my family, I guess," I said, "and moving away from home, and, y'know."

"Right on," said Harrison.

"It's kind of, y'know, an improv song to me," I said. "I've only played it live once, and it sounds so different on record. And I mean, I wrote it quickly, so."

"Is that good or bad?" Harrison said.

"To do it quickly?"

"Sure."

"I don't know," I said. "I didn't really think too much about doing it. I just started, and then I looked back and it was done."

•

Astrid pulled the studio door half closed and said goodnight to me, street light laid as a blade across her face. I clanged down the metal studio staircase and into the street and I heard the door clump shut behind me, and walked alone to the bus stop. I patted down my pockets for my Oyster card, and cursed as I realised I'd left my keys at home. I texted Rip to see if he was there to let me in, and he sent me a one-word reply. A piece of early blossom caught in my hair, which was growing out. I brushed off the pink petal, and watched it drift up and away, down the street.

•

Rip had been admitted to intensive care on New Year's Eve because he briefly stopped breathing during the ambulance ride to hospital. It had been close to midnight, around the same time I'd been trying to chat up that faceless girl at the Apollo. The voice on the phone on the first of January had told me that he'd "been mugged, or something," and where he was, and so I scrambled, half-pissed, guilty and stinking, to find him.

I got there and got shown to his room. His eyes came open as I entered, and shut again when I halted in shock at the state he'd been left in. The individual bruises on his face had melded, and gave his whole visage the appearance of a burnished dragon's egg. He seemed long and thin in his bed, limbs painfully askew, and his breath rattled like a sputtering engine in his chest.

I sat down and he told me what happened.

After he'd hung up on me in Hammersmith, he got back on the Tube without bothering to see if any of his uni mates were about, instead making his way home alone. Three guys followed him off the train at Stepney. He noticed them behind him – one called out to him as they came out of the station. When police asked Rip to describe them, all he could remember was that they were three men, all dressed in blue, and by the time they were taking turns to use his head as a football he was in no state to recognise anybody.

"It happened," Rip said, "so I guess it was inevitable."

I hugged him and shook with rage and sorrow and for it being all my fault as he emptily stared dry-eyed over my shoulder. The guilt made me want to die. As I broke down in front of him he kept on saying, flatly, "don't apologise."

Then we sat not really saying anything for about an hour, because there was nothing to say, and it hurt Rip's mouth to try and speak. By lying there he told me what I needed to know: I had abandoned my friend and it was him, not me, who'd been punished.

I looked around Rip's room; tinsel was listlessly draped around a stopped clock. They'd put him in here after taking him off the ventilator, which they'd put him on after using some kind of tube to suck the blood out of his lungs. He was breathing on his own now, raggedly. The air itched. The hospital staff had only just managed to reach his parents on the phone because they'd slept in after their New Year's party. They were on their way.

"I really wish you could fucking smoke in here," Rip said, and I said I would take him outside for a cigarette. I trundled him through squeaky-floored corridors in a wheelchair, one handed, running my other hand along the faded paint of the breeze block hospital walls.

When Rip was discharged a few days later his parents came to pick him up, and took him back to Brentwood.

"For the foreseeable," they said. I guessed that Rip had told them exactly what had happened, because they never really met my eye again after that.

•

Rip let me in, and without saying hello resumed his position at the kitchen table. He was poring over his uni ringbinder and a fan of lecture notes, and tapping at his laptop as I brought in the late February air behind me. His eyes flicked up at me briefly as I hung up my coat in the hall, and then he looked back down at his work. The bruises on his face had gone from black to blue to green to what they were now, a kind of a yellowy grey, mostly around his eyes, and he had some butterfly stitches on his cheek which they'd put in, after taking out the big stitches they put in in the first place.

"So, today was good," I said, stepping down into the kitchen. Rip didn't reply, just kept tapping at his computer. "Really fun. They seemed pleased, so."

"They? I thought it was just going to be you and *Harrison*." He emphasised the name every time he said it now, and had done for a while. The joke being, I guess, that I would bring up Harrison's name at any given opportunity, and he was mocking me for it. A couple of months ago, before everything, it would have been funny.

"Well, Astrid was there."

"Sure."

I sat down at the table opposite Rip. The silence in the house felt muffled, and the fridge hummed to my left, his right.

"What're you writing about?" I said, pulling one of his pages of notes towards me, which he pulled back distractedly without looking up, still punching one-fingered at his keyboard.

"Kant," he grunted.

"Was he a bit of a Kant," I said, lamely, and Rip didn't reply, and his frown deepened. "Died a virgin, you know," I went on. "And he did alright for himself. So maybe there's hope for you after all–"

"I'm working," Rip snapped. His eyes widened exasperatedly and I felt a swoop of anxiety in my stomach at the way he spoke to me, as I had the last time, and the time before that.

13.

Marta whacked me playfully on the head with a copy of my seven-inch single, which had come out the day before and which I was now seeing for the first time.

"I guess this means you're, like, famous now," she said. I grinned as I snatched it off her and ran my fingers over its cling-filmed cover. Astrid had chosen for the sleeve a close up photo of my face that she'd taken during the studio sessions: I was cobalt blue and my eyes were closed, and she'd said in her sincere and soft way that the shot looked like a beautiful death mask, and that it was perfect for my first release. I thought that Rip would laugh at that if I told him, if he were coming tonight. My name was printed above my head in spidery white lettering, and the picture and text were replicated on posters which were hung up around the store, with the words HARRISON DALBY LABEL LAUNCH TONIGHT underneath.

"How are you feeling about the show?" Marta said.

"Good," I said and the corners of my mouth pulled down, and she smiled and said it was going to be great. The label, which Harrison had decided to call Hem Haw – Astrid had shrugged when she told me – had got me an in-store show at Rough Trade East, and Marta and I had come down hours before to scope it out, and to see my new bit of wax on the shelf.

As I thought about everything my nervousness sent cold pangs to my chest, and my fingers tingled numbly as the day drew itself inexorably to the time of my performance. It was only my second show – it'd been, what, nine months since my first? Harrison kept on going on about how I should be "out there, doing it," but it hadn't even really occurred to me that I should still be organising my own things in the time that I'd spent elated about waiting to record with him. Plus I'd got side-tracked by everything during the weeks surrounding the New Year and hadn't been writing, and had instead just been robotically turning up to my shifts at Bean There, but now it was May and the buzz I could feel in the air made me swear to myself that I would finally do some work, do something again, not just wait and wait.

Marta had got back in touch with me around the time that I'd been recording with Harrison and Astrid, while Rip had been recuperating. I was surprised: it wasn't like we had any reason to talk to each other, and when I didn't hear from her for ages I guessed she'd lost interest in me after that first steer towards Jim Benson's place. But I came across her one day at the flat when she was visiting Rip, and we had a short and friendly chat and then she started to occasionally ask me to come to shows she was putting on, or she'd come and visit me at work, and I'd sometimes slip her free cups of coffee.

Our sympathies aligned in those brief blooms of conversation, and I found out about her, about her home town and her family who loved her, and about how she and Rip had bonded as trans kids in a big city, and how a budding romance had been uprooted by a mutual and sudden realisation that their attraction seemed only to come from a perceived similarity of situation, but that Rip was going through the strains of a change from which Marta was now far away, and she found she couldn't console him. She'd tell me these close things, things which Rip had never told me, and then she'd disappear, sometimes for weeks at a time. I was bewildered at first, but then discovered her long absences were because she was the sort of person who could breeze in and out of people's lives and make it seem normal and natural, and the warmth of her return made you forget how cold you'd been while she was gone, and I felt wanted. Then she'd go away again, the bright light of her presence suddenly shut off, and I'd be left stunned and blinking, blinded by the persistence of her in my vision.

Then the tech guy brought down the house lights, so that Marta and I were suddenly standing together in a pool of darkness between the lights of the street and the stage, and then I got called over to soundcheck. I was going to be the only performer that evening.

People began to descend on Rough Trade in twos and threes, tentatively alighting on the record shop's front steps like little birds, hopping haltingly through the door. I laughed when I saw Matt and Oggy from EIO shambling in: they both looked hungover, and clung to each other as they scowled at the room in their search for a glimpse of Harrison, who I knew they'd have come solely to see. Harrison himself had arrived, and was standing lordly over the merch stand, happily signing copies of both my record and his own LP that he was flogging. I watched as Matt and Oggy beelined right for him, colliding with an officious Astrid, who directed them to the back of a queue. I smirked and waltzed up to the table, wordlessly bypassing both them and the rest of the line, making sure they saw, and then leaned right into Harrison, interrupting his conversation with some well-meaning admirer. He looked up, seeming annoyed, and his expression didn't soften when he saw it was me. I walked away without saying anything, and hoped no one else was looking.

"Hey, Jude!" Matt shouted from the back of the queue, and I turned around and went over, slowly. As I approached I saw Oggy snigger at Matt's unintentional joke, but he straightened his face when I looked at him. As I came to a stop in front of them both, Matt said without smiling, "good to see you, man." He dithered over hug or handshake and ended up kind of cleaving himself to my arm, and we both laughed awkwardly as we came apart.

"How's it going?" I said.

"Good, yeah, yeah... Cool that you're, y'know." He gestured to one of the posters.

"Yeah, yeah, not a bad little gig to get," I said, my voice suddenly loud, oddly braying.

"I didn't know you were on Harrison's–"

"Top secret mate," I said, still sounding weird, and to my own horror I winked. Why was I being such a cunt? Oggy wasn't listening; he was peering over my shoulder, his attention still fixed on Harrison at the merch stand.

"Soo, yeah," I said, in a fried drawl, swinging my arms. Matt and Oggy looked at me.

"Maybe you should, erm," Matt started to say, with a nod indicating the stage.

"Right, yeah," I said, suddenly deferent, and found myself bustling away. Oggy said something behind my back, and Matt laughed.

More people came. Rough Trade staff drew the racks of records away, giving the massing audience a clear line of sight to the stage, and Marta jogged up to me in her jeans and T shirt and cute white pumps and said "Harrison's going to introduce you, and then you're on."

"Well," Harrison said into the microphone from the stage, his breath distorting his voice as he held the device too close to his face, "thank you all for coming, we are super excited to show you the fruits of our labours today, so, uh... yeah!" He paused as people huddled close to the stage's small barrier, and conversations subsided.

"Jude is going to play *now*, and then afterwards we will be signing the stuff, and, yeah. We've – Astrid from The Rayographs and I, and Steve, and everybody – have worked most diligently on this project, and we're very glad to show off the first artist to be added to the collection. Hem Haw, baby, welcome to you all."

I took this lack of formal introduction as my cue, and Harrison walked off to light applause and there was a singular wolf-whistle as I, single name Jude, Jew name Jude, four beers in, took the stage. I still hadn't taken Marta's advice and got a band together. Maybe that was my thing now. I heaved my new guitar over my shoulder and fumbled with the jack lead, and I think Astrid got onstage with me to help get me plugged in properly, and the stage lights burned into my shining forehead as I started up a new number called "Dead Man, In Love," which was kind of a rip off of a Sam Cooke joint, and had me doing falsetto "oohs" at its open and close.

I felt that audience locking-on feeling as I hit its highest note, I think people maybe didn't think of me as a singer, and when I proved I could do something other than bark they seemed to like me for it. "Thank you," I slurred into the mic as the song's final chord rang. People were invested in the whole situation of this label launch, and Harrison Dalby was sitting on the side of my stage, and so when I finished my song, the room erupted with cheers and applause. I remember thinking, "holy fuck."

I tooled around for thirty seconds having not really thought about what I was going to play, and still only having about seven songs, then I hit on one I'd learned for fun recently, that Rayographs number "Lighter To Bear." I felt Astrid's toothy grin from the back of the room like it was a searchlight, and I sang her words back to her. People didn't really seem to know it, but I was pleased to see that it had the same hypnotic effect when coming out of my mouth as it did hers. The crowd swayed.

More fiddling between numbers, and I fumbled at

machine heads before deciding to make it quick and call it quits up there, and there was a small but perceptible "wahey" of familiarity when I started up on "Freezin Rain" and I swore I saw a dowdy older couple near the front mouthing some of the words together. When the song clattered to its close a sincere cheer went up, and I bowed for the first time in my life before taking my leave to prolonged applause. Holy fuck.

•

Steve the label PR guy had his arm around my shoulder, and the tang of his sweat said he hadn't been to bed the night before, and he'd been passing around some legal high powder that was called, I shit you not, Gogaine, and I refused it but a bunch of his hangers-on were snorting it off their fists in the Rough Trade green room, which was actually a store room, and now they were all coming up on what looked to be a janky, jangling high.

"'Ere y'are, Jude," Steve said, his spittle flying as his Mancunian whine buzzed above the din. An iPod plugged into some little speakers was playing something from a new-wave record I didn't know. "Get that down yer neck." A beer landed in my hand, and I downed half of it straightaway with an agonised expression on my face.

Steve's bead-black eyes examined mine, flitting from left to right. I'd met him twice now: he was a fat little fuck, who'd apparently worked as a radio plugger and stuck to Harrison like glue when Harrison had first moved to London. I'd seen him perving on Astrid, and wherever he went he always seemed to bring with him a small coterie of young girls, sixteen- and seventeen-year-olds, who he'd attempt to impress by introducing to nobodies like me. He produced one of these young women by extending then retracting a tentacular arm, extracting her from a conversation she was having with a friend. He told me Rhiannon was an aspiring DJ and I shook her hand, and then before she could get away she was being bustled into a corner by the forty-something fatso, and I saw her fearfully laughing as Steve gave her bumps of the fake coke to do off his hand.

I turned away, and nodded in time to a plodding beat. My eyes opened and closed at the start of every bar. The room was cold in the absence of since-departed hangers-on, and people had stopped congratulating me in passing, and those left were now huddled in cliques in corners. I wandered back onto the empty shop floor. Matt and Oggy had finally made it to the altar of the merchandise table, I noticed, and envy prodded at my ribs as I watched Harrison garrulously entertaining them with some story or other.

Then into my field of vision swam a face I recognised but had not yet met, and the face said it belonged to Luke Leach. He was a writer for a music magazine that I'd heard of but not read.

"Yo," he said. He was about thirty, and one of those posh people who can't pronounce the syllable O properly, so it kind of came out sounding like *yew*. I accidentally mimicked him and then giggled to myself, and his smile froze for just a second before his confidence surely righted itself, and then he told me what he liked and didn't like about my show. While he talked I just stood there. He was drinking the same bottled beer as me, and then when he finished saying something and I couldn't even be bothered to say "mmhm" anymore, I lifted my bottle and smacked it on the top of his. His drink erupted in a spray of foam which flew up into his face, and then volcanoed down the front of his tan trousers, and his brownish unpolished brogues. I brayed with laughter, and hysterically he tried to join in as he patted himself vainly down. He looked up at me from a half crouched position, bug-eyed and with lager dripping off the stalactite of his chin. I looked around to see who had seen, and met only the eye of Gabriel from the Rayographs who shook his head and mouthed, "fuckin' 'ell, Jude."

•

Marta had given me a wide berth after the show so I could mingle or whatever, and I appreciated her letting me have my night, but I suddenly found I didn't want it anymore. I saw her leaning against a wall looking cool but forlorn, and I walked up to her and kissed her.

She kissed me back. Her tongue brushed mine and she put her hand on my waist and I felt small and pretty and then we came apart and her face turned to ash as she looked over my shoulder, and I turned to see Rip standing there alone in the middle of the emptied shop floor. We blinked at each other across widening space, and he turned and walked away.

14.

Summer in 2012 brought back from its trip round the world a fierce and relentless heat, which beamed down on London in an unblinking glare. Concrete council blocks seemed cracked from the bottom up and, at night, purple pavements sunk and swelled, the back of some exhausted beast. For the whole summer the windows of Marta's place in Bethnal Green hung open like panting dogs' mouths, and during the balmy nights I had found amniotic protection in her bed.

She and I had only been seeing each other for two or three months, but since then we seemed to have barely spent a night apart. She was twenty-six, I would soon be turning twenty-one.

One afternoon in July we awoke to the din of the street three floors below us, and white-hatted red buses vibrated by the open window, and we were bathed in peach coloured light, that rested like a petal on my tongue.

I felt Marta come awake seconds after me and we slithered in unison deeper into the bed, the outside of her sheets cool from last night and perfectly fitted around our unified form.

"Hello," she muttered and I said it back, and she kissed the back of my neck. We lay still for a long time, breathing in and out together. I drifted out of a half-spun dream as I felt her cock harden against my backside and I turned round to face her, and kissed her. We shimmied out of our underwear and kicked it from the covers, both naked now with our chests pressed together and I kissed her neck as she slowly massaged my cock with her left hand, and a moan escaped my mouth through the space between my lips and her soft skin.

"Open your eyes," she said, and we stared at each other as she tenderly stroked me. I put out a searching hand but she gently pushed it away and kept staring into my eyes as she touched me, and I looked away and she said "look at me" and so I did and then she slid down out of sight, and I gasped as she took me in her mouth. I came very quickly onto her fluttering tongue and she swallowed sweetly and reemerged, kissing my lips and pressing her face into my shoulder.

"Hello," she said again.

We got up and I made coffee, and we stood on Marta's balcony in lilac bedsheet togas and looked down upon the Old Bethnal Green Road, cradling our cups close to our chins in praying mantis poses. I slurped as she asked me what I wanted to do that day and after I swallowed I said, "stay in bed." She laughed and said "nope, we are getting up and being about, let me take you for food."

So we shed our robes and put on normal clothes and made our way down, down into the searingly bright street, which thrummed with the early afternoon heat and teemed with human traffic. She and I weaved in and out of the crowd and disappeared from each other behind costermongers' stalls, coming together again in the pavement's blank spaces to link arms, leaning our full weights against each other's shoulders.

We sat down at some cafe by the side of the road. I ordered fruit and some toast, and Marta had eggs. More coffee came, and a warm breeze sauntered around the corner we were sitting on.

"I spoke to Rip the other day," Marta said.

"Oh yeah?" I felt a sick swoop in my stomach. I'd barely spoken with Rip since he'd walked out of the label launch show in May. The thought of him over the past couple of months had filled me with a hot sadness that wouldn't cool, a feeling as though someone was forever wringing a wet towel in my stomach. "I didn't think he was talking to either of us," I said.

"Neither did I, I guess," Marta said. "But we ran into each other at a show last month, and it was just fine, you know?" I stared at her in plain silence and she ran her thumb over the knuckles of my left hand, which was laid on the table, half-wound into a fist. "Awkward, but fine. He mentioned you, you know."

"What did he say?"

"Just... that he's sorry the way things worked out," she sighed, "and that it's probably for the best anyway." Sick swoop again.

"For the best?"

"Well, he said that after New Year and... us, you and me," Marta said quickly and with a sigh again, "that there's just... y'know, people just change. And that's OK, and he and I are fine, and you and him are fine."

"We're not fine, though, are we?" I said, hating the plaintive ring to my voice. "He left without saying anything, barely, and we haven't spoken in weeks and weeks."

After the Rough Trade show, Rip had disappeared. For about a week I detected his presence at home solely from the jingling of his keys, and I couldn't tell if he was leaving or entering the house. Then I only saw him a few times, fleetingly as he passed through doorways, always pulling doors quickly closed behind him. That night at Rough Trade had been the last time we'd looked each other in the eye.

One afternoon I'd come home from work to find an email from him waiting for me in my inbox, and a bunch of his stuff in boxes in the hall, and his bedroom door was open revealing a stripped bed and bare walls, and open empty drawers. The email said he'd gone to stay with his parents until he could find a new place in London, because living with me was holding him back in his studies or something, and, because of the short notice, his parents could stump up his share of the rent until the year's lease ran out, and that he'd see me around, and good luck and whatever. He didn't say when he'd be back for the rest of his stuff. That night I sat on the floor of his room with my back to the closed door, glassy-eyed until I fell asleep only to wake a few hours later, sore and freezing cold.

"I think," Marta said with her mouth full, pausing to chew and swallow a piece of egg on toast, "that he'll be OK."

"I know *he'll* be–"

"*And* you, obviously," she said, raising her eyebrows, and smiling kindly. "You'll make it up, it's just probably good for you both to have some space from each other."

"If it was only space that he wanted," I started, suddenly irritated, a bead of sweat carving a path through my hair to the crest of my brow, "then he just should have just *said*, we're not nine years old, I would've happily–"

"If he'd said he wanted space from you, do you honestly think you'd have taken it well?" Marta said, kindly interrupting me again, and I looked down and frowned. "You'd probably have given him the same silent treatment he's giving you. Look," she went on, "I'm not saying that he's in the right, but look at it from his point of view: great things were happening for you at the same time that he got the shit kicked out of him, which is *no one's* fault apart from the cunts that did it," she said quickly as I raised my chin to interject, "and then you and me happened. Which I think no one expected." I smiled in spite of myself. "And he and I have a history, and... it was just all too much for him. It just probably felt easier for him to dip out of it, you know? I can understand that, even if I don't think it was the right thing to do."

Our plates were empty and a waiter cleared the table, putting down in front of me a bill which I hadn't yet asked for. The breeze threatened to carry it away and I grabbed hold of it before it blew off the table.

"I just think... I just *worry*," I said, "that after a certain point you can't take things back. I just worry I'm running out of time." Marta pushed her hand into mine.

"I think there's time," she said.

We got up and walked back to her flat through clearing streets.

15.

A pigeon shat on me as I stepped out my front door into the cold, damp street.

"Fuck," I said, setting down my guitar on the step and assessing the damage, a grey-white splatter on the shoulder of my leather jacket. I fumbled for my door keys and staggered back into the house, wiping off the offending excreta at the kitchen sink.

I was muttering to myself as I stepped back outside, guitar and rucksack piled high on my back, a plume of white breath escaping my mouth and rising into the air, disappearing. Then the morning's damp silence was broken by the rumble of an engine, and around the corner rolled a greying Sprinter van, carving its way through the fog. It honked its horn and pulled to a stop where I was standing at the curb. It was nine thirty. The passenger window rolled down and Astrid's head poked out of it and hollered "morning" and I waved as I ran to the back of the van to chuck in my stuff.

"Is that all you're bringing?" Astrid said as the side door whooshed open and I clambered in. Gabriel was sat on the seat behind the driver and I sat down to his left, and we shook hands as I strapped myself in.

"Yeah, why?" I said.

"Oh, no reason," Astrid said, cheerily. "I wish I could travel that light."

"Couple of pairs of pants and a T shirt and you're sorted, eh, Jude?" hollered Steve from the driver's seat, as he restarted the engine.

"Exactly," I bellowed back. I took a last look at my flat which was retreating in the van's wing mirror as we rounded a corner, to begin our journey north out of London. See you in ten days, I thought.

"Where are we picking up Harrison from?" I asked.

"He's already at the hotel, he took a train up last night," Astrid said after the briefest of pauses, turning to look out of the window through her tortoiseshell wayfarer shades.

"Right on," I said, and she didn't reply.

Steve was driving Astrid, Gabriel and me to the Trades Club in Hebden Bridge, where we were going to play as Harrison's backing group. Tonight was to be the first in a series of ten shows promoting a new book about Springs Eternal, and we were joining him in playing a mixture of Springs songs and his own solo stuff. Astrid was on bass and backing vocals, Gabriel was on drums, Harrison was singing and playing lead guitar and I was playing rhythm; the four of us had been rehearsing in Harrison's Hackney studio space for nearly three months since the end of July. My head had swum as I'd heard for the first time the chords of iconic songs like "Benjamin Christ" correspond to the movements of my fingers on my fretboard, and I had to remember to remember my upcoming parts, and not get caught up in staring at Harrison's mouth as that voice sang the words to those tunes I'd known for years and years.

On the road we lapsed into silence, the van vibrating as the M1 flashed past the window. Steve put on the radio which hissed and squawked as it tried to pick up signals from passing satellite towns.

"Oh hey," Astrid said, suddenly reanimated, rummaging in a bag at her feet, "did you guys see this?" She threw a magazine at me from her seat up front, and its pages rattled as it hit me in the chest and fell open onto my knees. "Page twelve." It was that week's edition of the *NME*. I turned to the correct page to see a double spread with the words "*DALBY SURROUND*" in a white, splashed-paint typeface over a huge, full-page picture of Harrison. He was standing in his usual clobber, huge T shirt, slack jeans and trashed trainers; three out of focus figures stood beyond his left shoulder in the middle distance. I was out-of-focus guy number two, the peach blob of my head adjacent to Harrison's teeth, which he had bared for the camera. He'd worn his horn-rimmed frames for the shoot, which he'd told me on the day was because he wanted people to think he was smart enough to have written a book. For the photo Astrid had stood to my right, Gabriel to my left.

"*Legendary alternative rockers Springs Eternal shocked fans the world over this year with the news that their latest album* Info Diet *would be their last before an indefinite hiatus*," the article began, "*but die-hard devotees of the New York four piece need not despair. Legendary frontman and guitarist*" – my eyes twitched at the repeat of "legendary," and roved to the top of the page to look at the name of the article's author – *"this coming week brings a selection of the band's classic tunes and his solo work on a UK tour, in promotion of his new book about the group*, Hell Is Empty: Being Springs Eternal. *The ensemble joining him on the road will feature Astrid Van Der Drift and Gabriel Owen (The Rayographs) and recent signing to Dalby's Hem Haw label, singer-songwriter Jude Hughes. 'It's a real privilege to be revisiting those songs, and reworking them for a new audience,' says Dalby, 55. 'I've loved working with new, younger musicians and giving everything a fresh feel.'"*

I smiled and put down the magazine. It was the first time my name or face had ever appeared in print, and the feeling of seeing myself obscured on a page was good and strange. It was me and not me: not just because I couldn't make out the features of my face, but because it referred to me in terms I'd never applied to myself, consciously and maybe otherwise. No one at the label had ever referred to me as a singer-songwriter before, I was just Jude. The band called me Baby Jude, sometimes; Harrison called everyone "baby".

•

I plunged my hands into the icy water of the Trades Club green room cool box, and a straggling bottle of beer floated to its surface to greet me. I cracked off the bottle's cap with my teeth and threw myself down into a fraying armchair, which faced the threadbare room from a corner. I was glad of a moment's respite in the room which was quiet.

The group and I had arrived maybe an hour before and were highly strung, having had to walk three quarters of a mile with our gear through the rain to the venue, arriving soaked to find a disgruntled Harrison complaining that we were late. He'd been pacing up and down the live room at the Trades

Club, a nervous sound guy in the background, Harrison's gear already set up on the small stage.

My name was called and I heaved myself out of my seat, and made for the live room. The Trades Club was an old union headquarters, and they still organised things like a cheap kitchen for local old boys, some of whom I squeezed past in the corridor between the green room and the steps that led onto the stage. I nodded with a tight lipped smile to Harrison as I walked under the lights, who nodded back without smiling and looked down at my beer bottle, saying "go easy on those, bud." It occurred to me that he hadn't tried to control my offstage behaviour when I was performing my own stuff, even when in his own studio; but now I was playing his tunes. I said that I would, with a nervous chuckle, and set the bottle down at my feet and began adjusting the settings on my guitar pedals, which were laid out in front of me. I'd been placed back and to the right of Harrison, unmiked and away from the lip of the stage. Astrid was tight close to his left, miked up and chanting "one, two, one two," over and over. Gabriel was rattling around on his drum kit, tightening this and that, adjusting the heights of his cymbals here and there.

"Alright," I breathed at him and his eyes rapidly flicked up to meet mine and then down again and he said, "yep, you?" I nodded my assent during a swig of beer, and then Harrison's voice said sharply over the PA, "Jude."

I turned, and it was my turn to check. I went through the usual motions, bashing out a couple of chords from one of my own songs.

"Something of mine, maybe," Harrison said at my shoulder and, flustered, I went "right, right," and falteringly began plucking out the opening strains of "Benjamin Christ" until the sound guy said "OK, stop."

•

A powerful stream of people burst through the venue doors at opening time, and pooled at the steel barrier which stopped them flowing onto the stage. Their babbling ceased as the lights went down and the supporting act strode on to begin their set. They were these three kids, all wearing pastel pink and blue costumes, and their set up was a drum machine, a synth and a guitar. I wondered how something like that had been booked to support Harrison, and later he told me after he'd had a few that he'd had nothing to do with booking them. It showed, because they were one of the worst groups I'd ever seen. They took minutes between each song to mess with their gear while the singer made bad jokes, which all ended with the words "right, guys?" Then they introduced a tune by saying "this song is about social justice," and I went to the green room for a drink.

Steve came in shortly after me, staggering under the weight of two beer crates. I helped him lower his load to the floor and we set about chucking the bottles into icy water. He told me that he'd had to argue with the promoter for the additional booze.

"They didn't bank on you comin' with us, did they?" he said, smiling malevolently, revealing his small and pointed teeth. I smiled back mirthlessly. My phone buzzed in my pocket to alert me to a text from Marta, asking me how everything was going. I wrote back that we had arrived, despite the rain and Harrison's temper. "*Oh dear,*" she said and I said that everything was fine. Then I wrote "*love you,*" and she wrote back "*kill 'em dead.*"

•

The reds and greens of the stage lights burned around

me like a cage, and I relied on animal instinct to find my place on the neck of my guitar which glistened through the veil of sweat raining from my brow. Harrison, Astrid, Gabriel and I were blasting our way at breakneck speed through the set, and five hundred people leapt into the air in time to our pummelling soundtrack, like grains of rice on top of a booming speaker.

Then there was silence, then screaming, then silence again and then a shriek of feedback and then Harrison gave Gabriel his cue and he counted off "Meat Cute", a new number from the latest solo record, and we hammered out the slow, sinister jam and the audience in their awe looked like kindling in a fireplace, burning white hot and ready to fly away above the flames. I was assuredly part of the Harrison Dalby quartet, these people were seeing me alongside their hero, and, as adrenaline coursed through me like a river in a thousand-year fast forward, eroding the banks of my veins and making my insides vibrate dangerously to the point of collapse, I felt so fucking alive.

The number ended, and a chorus of whistles sailed to the rafters. A sea of gleaming faces approved my presence, opening their mouths to roar at Harrison's recital of my name during role call at the end of the show. Astrid, Gabriel and I took our leave to howls and thunderous applause and watched, sweating joyfully from the side of the stage, as Harrison led an encore on his own and took a prolonged bow to let his fans' cries wrap themselves around him like gold ribbon. He came off, and the volume of the room seemed suddenly to drop as the house lights came back up, and he looked at us three standing there in his shadow, shivering with pleasure at this first undeniable success, and he said, slowly, "well, alright then."

He led us in single file back down the corridor, which was empty like a street that had been cleared for a visiting dignitary, to the green room, and when we got there he pulled us all a drink from beneath the ice and we clinked our bottles together in breathless victory.

"Day one, baby," he said, and we cheered.

At that moment the door flew open and a coterie of hangers-on flooded in, the dam of the stage barrier having broken: the sound guy and the support band, resourceful fans, the guys manning various arms of the venue's business, all came swirling around us. I was suddenly surrounded by three studious young music dudes, asking me a ton of questions, and in flex of muscle memory I tried to be like Harrison and cool in my response, but I was probably coming off as excitable as they were. They didn't seem to notice though, they just nodded their heads earnestly at everything I said.

The night passed in a fair haze and the booze seemed to run out very quickly, having been plundered by the small army of people cramming themselves into the room with the band. A few bottles had been stashed in my bag which I now inhaled, the polite part of the evening done, and I was submitting myself to an inevitable oncoming blackout. I noticed in double vision at around midnight when Astrid and Harrison took their leave, arm in arm, in their wake a group of fans disappointed that they couldn't get an audience with the couple. Somebody passed me a copy of my single to sign, and I scrawled my name along the edge of its plastic cover, and then drew a moustache on the picture of my face, and the person whose copy it was didn't laugh.

Steve shoved somebody in the back and they fell into my arms. It was a watery eyed boy, a cute kid of around seventeen or something, and he looked tremulously up at me as I reflexively bore down on his lips with mine. The room was now full of strangers, the band having bid goodnight to my back and leaving me to it, and people were cleaning up and I noticed Steve drag a few unhappy guests with him as he made for the van, which I knew he'd drunkenly plough back to the hotel.

The kid knew a number for a taxi and called it, and we fell into the car on top of each other, shrieking with laughter as we barrelled down dark and winding country roads. He smacked me on the head with a copy of my single which he'd bought, and our laughs were only silenced when we kissed.

We crashed through the door of my hotel room in the dark, and stripped each other with silent purpose, our breathing ragged and dangerous. Then we were both nude and I gasped with surprise as this little waif sat me on the edge of my hotel room bed and went down on me hungrily, his pale blue eyes shining up at me in sodium light, which through a gap in the curtains made the room orange and black and white. I pulled him on top of me and he shuddered and then I don't remember, I don't remember.

•

I awoke in an entanglement of limbs and stiff, strange-smelling sheets, and my mouth clacked open as I shoved a weight off me which was the boy, and he grunted as he came awake. "Hello," he rasped and I didn't reply, only got up and dressed, last night's sweat-encrusted clothes abrading my skin.

"Time to go," I said hoarsely, and the boy got up and dressed, and he backed his way to the door, averting his eyes from mine. Then as I got up to shut the door behind him, he looked up and craned his neck to kiss me, but I stepped back and pulled the door to forty five degrees, and said goodbye and he went away.

I heard my phone ringing behind me, and then there was the creak of an opening door and I peeked from my own room to see Harrison step into the corridor. He was holding his encased guitar and had his bag slung over his shoulder, and his eyes, red with sleep, locked onto the kid just before the kid disappeared round a corner, and then Harrison's eyes met mine.

"Morning," he said, and I said it back. "Good night?" I heard Astrid packing up her stuff in the room behind him. I said that it had been.

16.

I went downstairs to the hotel lobby to check out, handing my key card to a thirty-something-year-old woman in a turquoise uniform, who had braided hair and dark circles under her eyes. She was silent as I thanked her, and she looked with passing curiosity at my guitar which I hitched higher up on my shoulder as I made for the door. I sat on the hotel's front steps in the chill, my black jacket drawn around me like the wings of a bat, waiting for Steve to bring the van around. It was nine thirty. I heard the scuff of a footstep and turned to see Gabriel coming down the steps, and he sat down beside me. I winced behind dark glasses as he clapped me hard on the back.

"Alright," he said.

"Morning," I said. I drew a cigarette out of the crushed fag packet in my pocket, and fumbled for a lighter.

"Here," Gabriel said, lighting it for me.

"Thank you."

"Have fun last night?" he asked, lighting a fag of his own and blowing twin jets of smoke from his nostrils.

"Seemed to go down well," I said. In the distance I could hear the motorway. "Did it sell out in the end?" I asked. Gabriel shrugged.

"What time did you shake them off, in the end?" he said.

"What?" I said, sharply.

"What time did you leave," Gabriel said, laughing, blinking into the pale morning light. He scratched wearily at the young bald patch at the crown of his skull. "Those three lads looked like they were giving you the third degree."

"Oh," I said, realising that Gabriel was talking about the young guys who'd accosted me after the show, not the kid; I didn't know if Gabriel had even been there when the kid and I kissed. The night was confused. Guilt rose like a belch in my throat. "Yeah. They were OK. I was too pissed to really know what they were talking about. What time did you...?"

"Round about then," Gabriel said. "I'd had enough by about eleven thirty, long day and all that."

"Right, right."

Would Gabriel say anything if he knew? He and I weren't close. He didn't know Marta, either.

Marta.

I felt like the rest of the trip was going to be strange.

Gabriel and I pointed our heads towards the sudden familiar roar of the Sprinter van's engine, and through its dusty windscreen we saw Steve at its helm, fag dangling from his mouth, styrofoam coffee cup in one hand and he was steering with two fingers of the other. We sprang to attention and he rolled down the window.

"Morning ladies," he crooned, leering out, "how are we this morning?" We both groaned in unison, Gabriel's groan more cheery than mine, and Steve laughed, hopping out of the driver's door and dragging the van's sides open.

"Where's Ast– where's Harrison and Astrid?" I said as I got in and sat down, placing my guitar between my knees.

"They're taking the train," said Steve, pulling his door closed with a shunk and strapping himself in. "Alright for some, innit?" The van shuddered into life again, and went back on to the road.

•

I was thinking about my hangover, how I felt as though someone was trying to push my eyes out of their sockets from the inside. Steve was playing some shit on the radio, and Gabriel had a pair of drumsticks out and was tapping along to the track on the tops of his thighs. I shut my eyes, and focused on keeping them shut until we had completed the mercifully brief drive to Manchester.

"Don't look now, Jude," Steve said as we passed the Heineken factory upon entry to the city. I bared my teeth politely as Steve studied my reaction in his rear view mirror, and heaved myself upright in my seat and Gabriel, who had also dozed off in his chair, snorted and came awake.

We got to the venue. It was called the Night and Day Café. I had expected a similar scene to yesterday's arrival: techies and tour organiser types and merch stand guys and bar staff bustling around a busy live room floor, and Harrison pacing angrily up and down in amongst them all, but when we arrived through the venue's loading doors the place was empty. It took Steve venturing down a lonely corridor and bellowing before we detected the presence of another soul in the building.

A cry of "hiya!" echoed down at us from somewhere on high, and a sound guy who had been up a ladder doing something jumped down to ground level, to greet us. We introduced ourselves; after shaking our hands impatiently he asked where Harrison was, looked annoyed when we said wasn't here yet, and was walking away as he pointed us to the stage. Gabriel and I clambered up there, and started setting up.

My eyes felt like waterlogged tennis balls in my head. I knelt down and plugged in all my gear. I unzipped my guitar from its case, put it on and turned slowly on the spot as I played unamplified chords into empty space. Gabriel sat at the house kit and tested out its kick drum, which mournfully boomed into the blackness of the unlit room.

We soundchecked as best we could as half of a quartet, spending ten or so minutes messing around with variations of songs from the set, then downed tools and asked where we could dump our bags. I saw Steve leave the room hurriedly, talking rapidly into his phone.

"Light check time," warned the sound guy from his booth, "shield your eyes, people." A door banged open and I looked and was blinded as Harrison and Astrid walked into the room.

•

I slipped as I walked into the wings, and Astrid, walking behind me, caught me before I fell. She was laughing, and I was laughing as well. Gabriel and Harrison followed us, and the bellowing crowd behind us didn't quieten until long after we'd quit the stage.

The lights came up and the crowd could be heard retreating. Gabriel grabbed me jovially from behind and as I turned he held his hand up for a high five, and my hand missed his and nearly slapped him in the face and he shoved me, guffawing.

"You pisshead," he said. Over his shoulder I saw the shapes of Harrison and Astrid walking arm in arm down the corridor to another room, disappearing.

Then the barrier burst again and the band and I were ourselves up to our necks in people. Out of all of us, only Steve seemed still to be relishing this regular arrangement: I saw him place himself at the edge of the room, his black eyes moving ceaselessly over everyone who was entering.

A new gaggle of kids floated into view, looking exactly the same as the ones from the night before, and the night before that, and the night before that, and they were in front of me and fired off the same questions and I gave the same answers, but I was less drunk than yesterday so it was fine, I felt fine. The inside of this building and the hotel was all I'd seen so far of this city, the city I was in; it was the first time I'd been.

The room melted away and I was outside of it in a corridor and it was quiet, leaning my forehead on cool wall, and then a door burst open and out tumbled Harrison, holding Astrid in his arms.

"Can we hang out now?" she giggled as she fell further into him, and they kissed. I realised they hadn't noticed me standing there. The corridor lurched and I threw my head back and burped, and they both span around to see me swaying there. Astrid fussed over her hair and then turned away, and there was red rising from underneath Harrison's collar.

"What's up man," he said in a loud, flat voice.

●

In my hotel room I dozed with eyes half shut to the wet, soporific sound of cars passing under the window, and bars of orange crawled across the ceiling then down the wall, and slipped out of the room through the crack under the bathroom door. It was about two in the morning. Astrid and Harrison had taken the room next door to mine, and Gabriel was somewhere above us on the second floor. The windows were shut but the edges of the room fluttered somehow, and in the sound-baffled space my drunken breathing seemed loud, and close.

Drifting upwards into sleep I wriggled unhappily at a sudden wish to be in my own bed, and then felt a pang of fear as I thought about the empty house, to which I had to return in two days' time.

The show that night had been OK. The band was playing

well and we knew each other's movements and we could read Harrison's cues: he did this thing where he seemed to signal to the rest of us with the back of his head; we all dug it and locked eyes when he did it, smiling in unison at our joint understanding. But the audience had seemed for the first time kind of thin on the ground here, where we were, and from the stage I'd seen purple pools of floor dilating and then contracting as the crowd churned like the coming in and going out of the tide. Harrison hadn't given the crowd the whole "meet the band" spiel, and there was no encore.

"Good one tonight," I'd said to Astrid's back as we came out into the street. Everyone was leaving the party early. She'd turned to look at me searchingly and I'd caught myself staring at her mouth as she said, quietly, "you too." Steve brought the van around and she and I and the rest of the band got driven back to the hotel.

I couldn't sleep. My eyes flew open as the minibar fridge made sudden churning sounds, gurgling at me, and I rolled out of bed and onto the floor, crawling on my belly towards it and I opened the door, and a cascade of tiny bottles fell into my outstretched arms.

"Hello," I breathed stupidly, picking up a little Jim Beam, tearing off its head and downing its insides in a single gulp. Electricity wore through my veins, and I grabbed a second bottle and drank it down in one as well. I was laying prone after three, my head turned to normally-painful ninety degrees, and I then pressed myself up from the floor, and crashed backwards onto the bed. I thought about Rip and Marta and Astrid, and the kid, then about Dad for the first time in a long time, and then I fell asleep.

17.

In London, on the tour's last night, I was so pissed I could hardly play. Harrison had walked across the stage and I saw him come towards me in silhouette against burning white light, an all-enveloping eclipse. His right hand shoved mine out of his way and he seized hold of my guitar's controls, quickly fixing the technical problem that had bewildered me completely, and which had left me holding a uselessly buzzing instrument in front of tonight's thousand-strong audience. With a dribbling mouth I looked up at him as his face came into focus.

"There," he'd snarled, "now do your job and watch for the fuckin' count." He took his place back at the front and centre of the stage and genially said "well alright" to the expectant crowd who cheered at his return, and then he bellowed a count of four and we were off again, and I swayed on the spot, and tried to be good.

"Well, we got through it," Harrison said backstage, and we didn't clink bottles and he flopped heavily into an armchair, tossing his head and rolling his eyes, irritatedly flicking his hair from his face with both hands. Lukewarm lager trickled down my throat. Astrid and Gabriel were kind of huddled together near the entrance to the room, silently cradling their own drinks. I was stood in the dead centre of the room. I didn't know where Steve was, and there were no fans or tech guys or promoters or young cute boys, and the stereo that we'd been provided as part of our rider hadn't been turned on at all, and another bottle came into my hand and I blinked very slowly as the drink raised itself to my lips, and felt a wash of sleep come over me, and the room hummed.

I opened my eyes and I was alone.

I opened my eyes and I was being driven home.

I opened my eyes and I was in bed in my silent house, the ceiling of my room looking grey and domed and far above me, like a tomb. I rolled over in my half-sleep and remembered Harrison shaking my hand before he left me the night before, saying, "it was great working with you."

There had been talk of me doing a new single with Hem Haw after the tour was done. A week after I'd got home I sent Astrid a message about it, and she got back to me half-heartedly, telling me she'd be in touch. I replied with a message about still wanting to be involved and to thank her for taking me on the road with her, and setting up the whole deal, and then there was a back and forth between us that increasingly made me want to cry, and then I didn't reply to her last message which said, *"do I owe u something, Jude?"*

So I guess that was that. That is that, I remember thinking, over and over.

I would wait it out, I thought. But then it had been a month and a half, and there was still no word. Marta had offered to talk to Astrid to find out what was going on, and I'd had to hold myself back from begging her not to, and my body tensed with fear every time I thought of the two of them speaking ever again. Which they would, of course: but even though I was sure Astrid must know about me and the kid, I didn't think she'd tell. As each day passed, my unfaithfulness to Marta slipped further away, as did the tour itself, a dot of land disappearing over a grey horizon as I drifted further out to sea.

•

I woke up in bed, hangover lodged like a spike in my head, its tip touching to the very centre of my brain, and I tried to sit up but I had the shakes so bad I had to lay back down. Through a crack in one eye I saw there was no water, and I was thirsty and I thought, what am I going to do? I rolled onto one side and drew my knees to my chest and hugged them and felt weirdly lumpen, alien in bed, and then I realised I was fully dressed. I remembered I had clumsily stripped the night before so why was I, then I remembered it wasn't the morning after the night before, and then, as I shook and gasped and cried out because my head hurt so bad, I remembered what I could remember, and last night wasn't last night, and

Backwards, the real last night had gone like this:

I woke up in bed, wondering why I was still alive.

I woke up falling from a cab to the pavement, and staggered upright and puked over someone's garden wall, to the sound of the taxi speeding away. An upstairs light came on and shone on me and I turned and loped away as a shadow appeared in the window.

I woke up standing in the road, and, wind-whipped and freezing, looking wildly around, saw that I had somehow ended up on the Redbridge Roundabout, and everywhere was empty and neon lights were flickering and my bright phone loomed up towards my face and I couldn't read the screen but I stared and squinted and tried to make sense

I woke up with another tongue in my mouth, and from the dull roar around us I guessed we were in a bar and I laughed while kissing them back and cradled their head in one hand, trying to act romantic even though I was disgusting, and then I suddenly said I have to go and stood up and they looked so sad and said 'hey' sadly, but I laughed again and said bye and lurched forwards, across the pitching and rolling floor towards the door.

I was on a bus and settling into being semi-drunk. By the time I get there I'll be cooked, I thought. I'd been drinking since the morning and by the afternoon on a whim I was on a bus out of the city, to some thing, spending my last bit of money and not realising or caring what on, just going.

I woke up in bed and laughed as I picked up my phone

and sent a text to Marta that said *I'm going to kill myself today*, and she didn't reply.

•

Rip had left some old jeans in the bottom drawer of his dresser, and I was thinking about throwing them out. They were the acid-washed pair he'd worn with his matching denim jacket for that whole summer, a thousand years ago, along with his mirrored shades. I sat on his stripped bed, having just turned over his mattress for the new guy who was due to arrive today. The lease on the flat had just been renewed, and I had signed on to stay at the Stepney address for another year. I'd been living alone since May, and it was now December.

The low clouds that had covered autumn had kept in some of the summer's close warmth, like an oven that stays hot long after being switched off, but with winter they had dissipated, and the residual heat ballooned skyward and disappeared. Five early mornings a week I would stand in my kitchen before I went to work, cradling a mug of tea in my hands, watching its vapour mingle with my visible breath.

The doorbell rang. Still holding Rip's tatty trousers as I went into the hall, I opened the door and welcomed in David, the guy who was going to be my new housemate. He went to Central Saint Martins and was in a band, "like you," he'd said over the phone, and I hadn't bothered to correct him.

I'd posted an ad on Facebook about needing someone new to live with, someone sent it to him and he'd called me up right away. I'd looked up our mutual connections before we met for the first time, and he knew everyone, and therefore me, therefore my inactivity. Therefore my unceremonious dumping, therefore this, and that. He was nineteen and at six-five he towered over me, blocking out the grey December light as he lurched on convex limbs into my darkened hallway, and he dropped two large duffel bags and a guitar in a hard case with a thud onto the floor.

"Do you need a hand with your other stuff, or?" I asked, but he smiled with his catlike mouth and said that this was it.

"Travelling light," he said. He wore a kind of crushed faux-velvet suit and a permanent semi-sneer, and pointed black boots. His hair had been teased to stick up at the back, and his fringe with its blonde-gone-ginger dye job hung like rats' tails over his eyes. When he'd turned up to look at Rip's old room, he strode imperiously around the place, running his hands along the walls and countertops, as though testing for some quality or other. He asked me where the nearest music shop was. I said I didn't really know, but I could find out. At first I'd thought he was trying to impress me, knowing that I'd had a record out, but then I spent time with him, and I worked out it wasn't true. He'd smirked when I asked him if the bills were within his price range, waving away my question with the lit cigarette he always dangled from his hand, and asked me when I wanted his deposit, "and all that stuff." I said any time before he moved in. He paid me, and moved into Rip's old room.

I took him to the kitchen and made us both coffee, and he sat at the table, and lit a cigarette. I pointed out the cupboards where he could put his food, and showed him how the washing machine worked, and where could put his laundry basket, next to mine. As I spoke he stared vacantly into middle distance. The great dark circles around his eyes accentuated his face's pallor; the tendons in his neck jumped when I slammed the door of the washing machine shut. I sat down with him at the table.

"So, like," he said, "you work in a coffee shop?" Yep, I told him. "And that's like, your job?" Yes. "I thought you were a musician," he said, with upward inflection. I am, I said.

"Huh."

"You play too, though," I said, nodding to the hall,

where he'd propped his guitar up against the wall.

"Yeah, yeah," he said, "my group's playing next week at the Victoria, if you wanna come." He dug in his jacket pocket and produced a grubby flyer, and handed it to me. Under gothic-style writing announcing the debut of The Smiling Backstabbers were pictured David and three other kids in David identikit, matching him down to the faded bleach in their fringes. The gig was advertised as free, and no other acts were listed.

"Your first show?" I asked, and he nodded, picking sleep from his eye. I waited for him to tell me more but he demurred and we sat in the humming quiet of the kitchen, neither of us able to think of anything to say. His eyes darted up and met mine and I smiled, and then they darted back down again. I said I had to go to work, and he stood up at the same time as me but seemed not to understand why, and he took a half step in no direction in particular. I told him to text me if he needed anything, and he didn't reply, just turned weirdly on the spot to stare out of the kitchen window. I swept up Rip's jeans from where I'd left them on the counter and threw them into my laundry basket, grabbed my keys, and then went to work, leaving my new housemate in my flat by himself.

•

One night in late December, David and a pack of his friends were cavorting around the flat, partying with panic-inducing proximity to my room, where for the past hour Marta and I had been trying to sleep.

He and I had been living together for three weeks, and only once had he asked me if I was OK with his friends coming round, and he'd taken my one yes to mean that they were all invited in perpetuity, to rampage back and forth from his bedroom to the kitchen, endlessly piss on the toilet seat and bathroom floor, and smoke what I discovered to be heroin just about everywhere else. I kept on finding little burnt pieces of tin foil scattered across the floor, and once stepped on a jagged piece of it in bare feet and it sliced a deep cut into my big toe. Marta told me that apparently smack made you puke the first time you did it, and I told her I didn't need heroin for that, and so I'd steer clear. She laughed and said, "good boy." In the mornings the roar of the kettle was often accompanied by a lingering, sickly-sweet smell, and I had become accustomed to blackclad bodies draped across my kitchen table before I went to work.

"Do they *ever* go to sleep?" Marta asked me, her head on my chest as we lay together in bed, as a pervasive and threatening droning, David's music, seeped through the wall.

"Nope," I said. "They'll be up *still* by the time I get up for work, and they'll be up still by the time I get back."

"Doesn't he go out?" Marta said.

"Not really," I coughed. "He's meant to be studying, but I think he's been into uni once since he's been here. Don't think money's a problem, either."

"You surprise me."

"The other night," I said, voice cracking, "he brought back maybe five, six people."

"Mm," Marta said, listening with her face pressed into my shoulder, her left leg nestled in between my thighs.

"And they didn't know I was in. And obviously they start talking about me, or at least I heard my name a bunch of times. And you know that thing of, like, you want to say something, but you also want to hear what they're going to say?"

"Yeah..."

"Well I couldn't make out what they were going on about over the fucking shit music they were playing, but then I heard David go, um, 'seriously, I'll show you' and then I heard a few of them coming towards my fucking room and I'm in bed, naked, obviously–"

"Obviously," Marta said, a grin in her voice.

"–and so I just thought 'fuck this' and got on top of my covers, on my back–"

"Still naked–"

"Yeah," I said, "and pretended to be asleep." Marta snorted. "So the door opens, and they're coming into my room," I said.

"Unbelievable," she said.

"And so – yeah, I know – so, fuck knows what he wanted to show her, and it's probably not the first time he's done it, but some girl who he's sent in *ahead* of him comes in, and I can see her bumbling about, and she switches on the light–"

"Unbe-*fucking*-lievable–"

"–and the fucking look on her face, when she saw me lying there, oh my god." Marta guffawed and called me gross, and said that that would teach them to snoop where they weren't wanted but seriously, I should get a lock on the door, and we flinched as the door handle of my room rattled, for the third time that evening, as someone started to come in.

"Fuck off!" Marta roared, and the rattling ceased, and we heard heavy boots thumping down the hall in search of some other private space to invade.

I leaned across the bed and turned off the bedside lamp, and Marta and I huddled close together, in wait for sleep. Then my eyes flew open in the dark as I heard the opening bars of "Freezin Rain" come on over the stereo and Marta shifted uncomfortably next to me, and then the record was shut off as quickly as it had come on and I heard David's voice whisper "no, don't," which was followed by the cackling laughter of a voice I didn't recognise.

18.

The same ten or so carols were on a loop at work. Bea had tried to make Sarah, Euan and me wear those headbands with felt reindeer antlers attached, and we had repeatedly refused, and she had angrily cried while putting up tinsel around the espresso machine.

Howard and Danuta came by. They were passing and came in to wish me a merry Christmas. They gave me a card, which was also signed by their daughter. There was a picture of a gingerbread man on the front. I smiled and thanked them and they went away after buying coffee, and then I never saw them again.

•

On the twenty first of December 2012, at eleven minutes past one in the afternoon as I was sitting, demobbed at the kitchen table, staring at the faded red stain on the wall and hoping that David's latest disappearing act would at least leave me in the flat by myself for Christmas, Dad called to tell me that Mum was dead.

Thickly I wondered how he had got my number as I sat there in dumb, ringing shock.

"Hello?" he said.

"Hello," I whispered back.

"Her neighbour found her last night, she saw the front door standing open and let herself in." When was the last time I had heard his voice? "She called an ambulance but it was–" He stopped, and swallowed, then continued. "Too late by the time they got her to hospital." I waited for confirmation of my terrible suspicion, and it came. "It was him," Dad said.

I had known Mum had been seeing someone new for a while. In a picture that Two had shared online I'd seen

Mum sporting what looked like a fading black eye, and so I had figured out that this guy must have been using her as a punching bag. And then I got a text from Three one time, saying that she'd had to drive Mum to hospital for a broken arm, and she wouldn't say how she'd done it, but I knew, and I didn't do anything, and now she was dead.

With sudden searing clarity I remembered her at home and her desperation, the sound of lonely gasps behind doors pulled to. She had made a bid for freedom, and it had killed her. She had been gone, but now she was gone forever.

I gasped as though suddenly submerged fully clothed in ice water and I couldn't breathe, and tears splashed with tiny *thok-thok-thok* sounds onto the wooden table. On the phone, Dad waited for a pause in my sobs.

"You're coming home for the funeral," he said.

"When is it," I said, my voice tiny in my chest.

"I spoke to the people this morning," Dad said. "It'll be the twenty-ninth, if everything gets sorted in time."

"What about–"

"We don't know where he is."

•

So I went back to the house where I grew up. I came through the back door into the utility room and I'd forgotten that smell, muddy trainers and lino and washing powder, and I slipped my shoes off and stepped in socked feet into the kitchen where I had walked for so many miles in circles, a million years ago. The overhead lights burned down on bright and clean countertops under black windows, and I remembered hours spent idling by the toaster, and peering unseeing into the fridge between meal times. I remembered Mum coming home once and going to the bread bin to find that somebody had taken the last slice of bread without defrosting a new loaf, and she'd burst into tears.

I burst into tears. At the sound of my crying, One, Two and Three glided silently into the kitchen, very tall now, and as I turned they wrapped their arms around my neck, shoulders, waist, and the four of us stood warm together in our bright new grief, and when I finally opened my eyes and they had let me go I saw Dad through my veil of tears, standing small in the doorway, looking expressionless at his four mourning children. He walked towards our little huddle and put his arms around us slowly, shaking, and I convulsed at each one of his strange, racking sobs.

The five of us sat at the old dining room table, my sisters and I in the same places we used to occupy as kids, Dad at the head, Three at the other end, One and Two next to each other and me on the other side. We looked anywhere but Mum's empty chair, which was next to mine. Dad had prepared some food for us to eat and placed it on apologetic plates in front of each of us, but I couldn't see or taste whatever it was that I began mutely shovelling into my mouth.

I found myself alone at the table with the sound of running water coming from upstairs, and as Dad passed through the dining room from the kitchen he banged his knuckles against the door on his way to bed, and turned off the light and I sat for a long time in darkness.

I hauled myself to my old room, which smelled like carpet and had not been altered since I'd left however long ago, apart from some boxes full of Dad's stuff that had made their way down from the attic. I laughed in shock at a picture I had of Harrison hanging above my bed, and wondered how I had totally forgotten that it was there. I even remembered in sudden flashback taking it out of the middle of an edition of the *NME* one day after school, and I'd felt smug pride in liking Springs Eternal when no one but me and Rip even knew that they existed.

I got into my old bed, which was cold. I closed my eyes and as Harrison's portrait stared down at me from above like Jesus fucking Christ, the last thing I remember thinking was that I wished I wouldn't wake up. Sleep closed over me like the end of the world.

19.

For one blank and blissful moment as I came awake under my childish bedclothes, I didn't remember the events that had carried me there the day before. Light stung my eyes though they were shut, and I felt dehydrated and groggy, despite the fact I'd gone to bed sober for the first time in I couldn't remember how long. The air felt close and condensed, and I smelled my night sweat clinging to the sheets. As my eyelids drew themselves apart, the memory of yesterday's wretched journey to Brentwood trickled back into my brain and I heaved my legs over the side of the single bed, and pulled back the covers. My feet thunked to the floor. I tilted my chin towards the pale sunlight which was being posted through the slits in the blind, and my eyes roved wide over my old room's faded walls. I got dressed and went downstairs.

One, Two, and Three were sat in their places at the dining room table, heads bowed over empty breakfast plates. It was nine thirty. I said good morning and their eyes came up to meet mine and followed me as I took my seat. We had not been together in a room in over two years, and we had grown accustomed to knowing one another by our absence, and I felt strangely lumpen and uncertain in their presence.

We sat together in silence for a long time, and then the silence was broken by a thump from upstairs as Dad came awake, and all three girls opened their mouths at the same time to say something, and looked at one another to decide who should speak, and it was quietly decided that it should be One:

"Jude," she said, and I said what, and she said, "Dad said we have to go shopping for funeral clothes today."

"OK," I said.

"Unless you have a suit," Two said. I looked at her, puzzled, and she said, "Dad didn't know if you had a suit or not." I said that I didn't and she said "oh" and turned her eyes back to her empty plate.

"He said he thought you'd have one," said Three.

"I've never needed one," I said.

"Well, he said he'll get you one."

"OK." Number One picked up a butter knife, and put it down again.

"They found her with her phone in her hand," she said. I said nothing. Two and Three said nothing.

I noticed a tear fall from my left eye, and then my right. *Thok, thok.* I wondered if I had had my phone on me, but reminded myself I hadn't known, she hadn't placed the call.

I stood up without purpose at the same time as Dad entered the room. His blue eyes were like flint and he'd just shaved his face, I could smell his aftershave and his chin looked scraped, hardboiled.

"When you're ready," he said gruffly, and we went into the hallway and rustled into our coats and waited for him by the front door, and my ears pricked up at the sound of his jingling keys.

•

I forgot about Marta. I only thought to tell her what had happened on the day after I arrived back in Brentwood, such was my surprise at being teleported to my childhood home. She called me in the evening, after One, Two, Three and I had come back from listlessly traipsing around the high street and I had been bought a suit off the peg, and the girls had selected pretty and near-matching black dresses, and nice shoes which I knew they'd feel too sad to wear ever again.

Marta wept with me down the line and said could she come to see me and join me at the funeral, and we cried because she couldn't, but I told her I was coming back.

"I know you don't feel like it now," Marta said thickly when we had found our voices again, "but you are going to be alright." I nodded childishly, forgetting she could only hear me. "Not the same, different. But alright."

"She tried to call me," I said. "She tried to call me, the night she died."

•

On the morning of the twenty-ninth we got picked up from Dad's house by a black limousine, and I was dressed in my new black suit and out of the car got three long coated, corvine men in tall hats, and there was another car in front of that one and my Mum was in a box in the back of it, dead.

I was afraid and blurred my vision on purpose as I walked past her. I got into our car and sat in the middle, and Dad got in the front seat with one of the men in hats driving, and my three sisters squeezed into the two remaining seats either side of me. We got driven through Brentwood to the church and I saw an old guy see us trundle by as he came out of his house to pick up his milk off his front step, and he stood up stock still like a soldier with his head high as we passed.

"That's nice," Three said, in a faraway voice. It was nine thirty. I really needed a drink. The town came by in a grey-green blur.

The cars all pulled up, and my family and I got out onto cobbles and clip-clopped through the graveyard gate and into the church. My grandparents were stood by its entrance, the four of them in a row, staring straight ahead at nothing. My Dad's parents were thin and papery-skinned, in dull brown-greys; Mum's parents were large and pink, like balloons draped in bright shades of black. A man in robes appeared and shook my hand and everyone else's hands, and then I went over to the car to help bear Mum's coffin into the church, where words would be said over it before we took it outside to bury it. Two of the men from the funeral home, some cousin, my Dad, and some other guy and I heaved it from the hearse onto our shoulders, and about-faced in a very small stepped shuffle, and then walked slowly with it into the church.

The small crowd of mourners parted for us like fern fronds as we approached and placed Mum down, in her box, in front of the altar. The vicar stood aside as we placed the coffin down. He was small with white hair and I asked Dad later who he was and he said just the vicar of that church, our local one that we'd never gone to and he didn't know us but it was local, so where else would we bury her, and your grandparents are going to be buried here too, so where else would we bury her.

I drifted backwards to a front pew to be alongside One, Two and Three, where we sat with Dad, and his tiny parents sat with us and we couldn't help huddling together in the gloom. Mum's parents took the front row on the other side of the room, and the wooden pew creaked loudly as they sat. Their other grandchildren, my cousins, some of whom I'd only met once or twice, and some not at all, gathered around them. Other mourners drifted like fog through the door and silently took up space, an unsure and glistening presence behind. I turned, I couldn't make out anyone's faces. I turned back to the front of the room. The vicar started speaking.

"We are gathered here today to celebrate the life of Suzanne Jane Hughes," he murmured, "who has been taken up into the bosom of Christ. She was a devoted and loving mother to her four children, Emma, Jude, Magdalena, and

Hannah, and will be dearly missed by we who remain here on Earth. She was born in 1966, the daughter of Bernard and Shona, and grew up in Chelmsford where she studied at Boswell's School, and went on to read History at Swansea University." He cleared his throat, and turned over the piece of paper he was reading from. The front pew where Mum's parents were sat creaked again, loudly. I didn't know that Mum had gone to University. I knew Dad hadn't.

"She met her first husband Robert while working at his printing business," the vicar continued, "and soon after the couple married they began raising a family together." He went on about Mum some more for a bit, but not for long. He finished reading some Bible verse, and as he said "Isaiah fifty eight, eleven," I felt Dad lean across to say something to Two, and my head half-turned because I wanted to tell him to shut up, but before I could say anything, there was the very loud sound of crunching wood, and my head whipped around to see my Mum's parents suddenly dropping out of sight as their combined weight broke the church pew on which they were sitting.

Everyone stood up to look. One, Two, and Three clamped their hands over their mouths, Dad grabbed two fistfuls of his hair; I stared. I looked to the Vicar to see how he would make everything carry on, but he was just looking at everything that was happening, all these strangers, and calmly smiling.

•

Me and Dad and the other four people I didn't know picked the coffin back up and took it to Mum's grave, just a little way up a path from the church. It was eleven o' clock. Some more words were said, she was lowered down, down; a small pile of dirt passed into my hand which I threw into the hole in the ground.

In somnambulism the mourners turned and made their way silently up the path, and I looked back and saw the crowmen shovelling dirt into the hole they had made. The low winter sun hung like a coin in between their tall hats and glistened the gathering sweat on their brows.

I looked back at the path and the congregation had suddenly disappeared, and Rip was coming towards me with crunching steps.

20.

"I got the train down, soon as I heard," Rip said. "Stayed with my parents last night."

"Marta told you," I said. He nodded. There was no trace of a bruise on his face; it had been a long time.

"I'm so sorry, Jude," he said evenly. It was strange to hear in real life a sound I thought permanently committed to memory. I said that it was alright. I walked towards him and then came to a stop, and then we were ten feet apart. His hair had gotten longer. He was a little less skinny than before, and the black clothes he hung off his bony frame looked new, or at least not frayed. He came closer.

"How was the service?" he asked. I said that I didn't really have anything to compare it to, only that it seemed the same as a wedding, but sadder. I told him the story of the pew breaking, and my grandparents hurriedly dusting themselves down and struggling to their feet, their pink faces pinker, and the concerned congregation crowding around them as they shooed everybody away with furious embarrassment and only wanted to sit back down, but couldn't risk breaking another bench and so stood in plain sight for the rest of the service, heads bowed.

"Holy shit," Rip said.

"Weird day," I said.

We blinked at each other and both smiled small smiles

and I was very tired, and there was the yawn of a car driving off somewhere. People were making their way to the wake already. It was at some hall down the road, and I guessed Dad hadn't thought to tell anyone to wait for me. I'd walk.

"Why'd you come?" I said to Rip.

"How could I not?"

"We haven't spoken in, what, six months?" I said. And even then not properly since, well."

"I know," he said, with a profound breath out that I breathed in, and it wound itself like a fist around my heart. "But, look man," he began.

"Stop," I said, and Rip looked at me and stopped. "Thank you for coming. And I'm sorry for everything. I'm glad you're here, and everything went to shit anyway, I've been having a shit time, so it's not, like, y'know, and I'm sorry. I'm sorry, I'm so sorry."

"Jude–"

"I just, I fucked you over, with everything, I was, I just–"

"Jude."

I stopped.

"I'm here," Rip said. "OK?"

"OK," I said.

"So that's that. OK?"

"OK."

"And as for all the fucking mess," he said, "everything that fucked us both up for a whole year... Maybe in another life, you might have something to show for all of it, and it might have been somehow worth it. But whatever happened, I'm here."

I looked at Rip's face. Hard-trained, to give nothing away. A film of tears covered my eyes and I was bored of crying, and I angrily wiped them away and then shudderingly breathed in very deeply.

"Will you come to the thing?" I asked, my long since

self-anaesthetised fondness for Rip suddenly crashing in on my heart in massive waves, now that he was here. He put out his hand and I walked towards it and took the tips of his fingers with the tips of mine.

"Come on," he said.

A cloud overhead revealed the sun, and I screwed my eyes shut as I was blinded by the bright, late morning. Rip and I turned and walked together down the path and into the churchyard, back past the graves, pausing to laugh at stones bearing funny names. Rip's laugh today was a gentle peal, and he squeezed my hand as we walked. The damp grass bounced under the soles of our feet.

●

I didn't know most of my extended family. I hadn't seen them at all since leaving home, and before that only sometimes, at Christmases and things.

At the village hall where the wake was being held, cousins, uncles, aunts, old colleagues of Dad's and forgotten family friends milled around a table bearing white bread sandwiches on paper plates, and a makeshift bar propped me up as I bore down on the Famous Grouse that some kind soul had supplied. I picked up the bottle and poured myself a large glass, and threw the drink into my mouth and felt each muscle of my pharynx wilfully tighten and send it down, down my throat and into my stomach, where it sat and sourly burned.

Rip was with me at the bar, one arm around me with a hand on my shoulder, the other hand fingering a book in the inside pocket of his jacket. He was a protective force, a layer between members of my family who would otherwise have come up to me and quizzed me about me, and I was very very glad of his presence, and I revelled in being silent. Everyone in the room passed in sequence to stare at him, not seeing me, and I liked being invisible.

Favourite songs of Mum's were playing. There was the sound of a record scratch and Bowie's "Golden Years" came on, and with sudden, giving force, like a needle piercing skin, I was reminded of her dancing to that tune in the kitchen, alone and smiling with a mixing bowl, and she saw me watching and, laughing, dragged me onto her dance floor and we danced together, my nine-year-old head pressed against her stomach, and her stroking my hair.

Then I thought about another time, maybe it was the same year, when I was lying in bed and listening to the murmur of the TV downstairs, almost asleep when I heard her softly insistent voice call my name and my eyes came open.

"Jude, Jude," she was saying. "Jude, come and look at this." I'd got out of bed and gone downstairs in my pyjamas, and into the living room which looked different from how it did during the day, golden, forbidden. Mum was supine on the pale sofa, a glass of wine held aloft, loosely by her fingertips. She'd smiled lazily at me and drawn me to her, and said "you'll like this."

An old sitcom was on the TV: a man was standing in the street, shouting at his red car which wouldn't start, and as he walked out of shot Mum said "look, look," in a hushed voice and my eyes bulged when the man returned with a tree branch which he used to furiously thrash his broken-down vehicle, and Mum laughed as I laughed and squeezed me and kissed me on the cheek.

As the music played at her wake I poured myself another drink, and drank it.

Then the music stopped as the sun's light dimmed in the village hall windows.

I blinked and the room was dark, and Dad was in a corner fussing over something's wrapping, and One, Two and

Three were nowhere to be seen, and Rip and I were sat on the floor with our backs against the bar. I cradled yet another glass of whisky in my right hand, and gripped the bottle tightly in my left. I pulled a loose cigarette from my pocket and lit up, and when the smell of smoke reached Dad's nose he turned and stared hard at me for a second, but then thought better of whatever he was going to say and turned away. Rip lit one too, and our smoke drifted towards the ceiling from our mouths, and twisted into a braid, disappearing.

The wake was over. That is that, I remember thinking. Everyone had gone, and nobody said anything about what would happen now.

•

Rip and I walked out into the village hall carpark and I dragged the now empty whisky bottle behind me like a longsword, and he put the book he'd been reading back in his pocket. I said Dad would give him a lift to the station later, but he said he'd walk.

"I have work in the morning, so I'd better get going."

"OK," I said.

We embraced and his cool forehead briefly rested at the base of my neck, and then he turned, and left. I watched him as his small figure descended into the distance to the road which bore him back to the station, where a train would take him to London.

I heaved the heavy bottle up into the air, and watched it sail above my head and hang, glowing, before it fell with a bright crash onto the ground. I stared at the shattered glass for one, two, three seconds before feeling a chill, and going back inside.

21.

It was January 2013 and I was at home, sitting at the kitchen table. Grey daylight reflected off the blade of a butterknife, and concentrated in a dance on the ceiling.

The days were getting longer. Mercifully, David had left me alone after I'd returned home from Brentwood. I was sure he'd rustle through the door at some inopportune hour pretty soon, but for a good week now I'd not heard a peep out of him. In his absence I'd swept the floors and binned any half-empty bottles of spirits he'd left lying around, and trod carefully in anticipation of jagged metal nestling in the hallway carpets. I found none; the house was clean.

My phone rang, and buzzed towards my hand across the table. I answered. On the line was some kid, calling me up to offer me a gig. I wondered why he wanted me and how he'd got my number, but didn't ask. I hadn't played solo since the Rough Trade thing.

"Um," he said.

"So," I said, after he'd told me that he had a club night, well, a fanzine, but a club night based off of the fanzine which, um, features, um, bands featured in it, "where were you thinking of doing it?"

"There's this place," the kid gulped. His name was Joe, I think. "It's called The George Tavern…"

"Yeah, I know it," I said, with a tired smile.

"Great, so, um," Joe said, "it's next month, and it'll be you and two other bands and DJs, oh and, um, my band."

"Who's your band?"

"We're called, um, Ex-Giant," he said and laughed sheepishly, and I said it was a good name. He told me that they played late-eighties-New-York-inspired stuff, and that he thought I'd be a good fit as a headliner. His group was going to open, he told me, but they'd be billed as main support so more of their friends would come down, and of course people's sets would be pushed back, for maximum audience numbers, and stuff. Good one, I said. Rip's voice said "ha!" in an echo, in my head.

Joe was going to give me fifty quid, and I was glad of it, and I told him so and said thank you. He thanked me for agreeing to do it, and asked if there was anything else I needed. I said that there wasn't, gave him my email address and told him to keep in touch. He said that he would. I hung up.

"Who was that?" Marta said as she came into the room, scrubbing at her wet and knotted hair with a towel. It was four in the afternoon, and she was getting ready for work. Her bare feet left little imprints of condensation on the kitchen tile.

"Some kid, putting on a night at the George," I said. "Got a show to get ready for, I guess."

"How nice," she said at my side, smiling and bending to kiss me, and I kissed her back.

•

Euan quit working at Bean There, and the day after he'd gone I noticed that his "Shoulders Down" sign had been taken down. Then I looked up and saw Bea remonstrating with a cleaner who'd shown up late, and hadn't finished mopping the floor before customers began to arrive.

"It's not good enough," she said, her eyes madly rolling in her head, "you've got. To be. On time." If she could get away with it, I was sure she would've been poking the guy in the chest in time with her speech.

"Sorry, sorry," he whispered, clutching a wrung mop which slowly dripped water onto the floor at his feet. He was about forty; I didn't know his name. "Sorry, sorry."

"Yeah, well," Bea said, with a writhe, pushing her frizz

of ginger hair out of her eyes and standing a foot shorter than the man whose job she was threatening to take away, "don't be sorry. Just be on time." The guy dumbly nodded and shuffled off to finish up, and when he left later that morning he looked at me over his shoulder and mouthed "bye."

Bea was very present on the shop floor after that, and at one point came pacing past the counter and shouted "Christ!" into occupied space and several heads turned, and she looked at me and sneered "what are you staring at?" Fuck this, I thought.

I gave my notice the next day. I told Sarah I'd be leaving, and she asked me what I was going to do next and I said I didn't know, which was true. When I told Bea, she said "well, I can't say it's been a pleasure," and I laughed and shook her hand.

Later that week she told me I'd have to train my replacement for a day, and that he'd be coming in later. My back was turned as Sarah showed him through the door and into the back room, and as he was getting ready, Bea bustled past me, saying "the fucking idiot's turned up in sandals." There was a shuffling sound behind me and I turned to face my replacement, who it seemed had bothered to shower for the first time since I'd met him, but looked hungover as always, and was still wearing a T-shirt adorned with some pretentiously obscure band on the front.

"Hey, Jude," Matt said. Bea laughed nastily as she walked off the shop floor, returning to the back room.

•

Just days before the show I decided to try and write a new song. The stuff I'd recorded with Harrison felt very old even though I'd barely played any of it live, and I wanted something new that said something about what had happened over the past year, to document it, and to put it away. I would include "Freezin Rain" in the set, and "Glacial Goodbyes," but I had to remind myself that I could still write, barely having picked up a pen, let alone a guitar, in months. I'd also decided to include covers of "Benjamin Christ" and "Lighter To Bear", as some kind of goodbye to Harrison and Astrid and Hem Haw, or maybe a sort of talismanic charm – I don't know. It felt important to do it, anyway. I liked my versions of their songs, too.

I sat cross legged on the floor of my bedroom, the neck of my new guitar resting on my left thigh, digging my knuckles into the carpet and trying to think of how to put it. I suspended a pen over a blank sheet of paper, and listened to my breathing. I heard the sound of water dripping from a tap, and closed my eyes. The pen placed itself on the sheet, and began to move.

The blood of my father
Gushes from my head
She's there and so bored.
I hate the weather,
I think I'd rather be
Somewhere underwater

Good luck to Marta
She's forgetting me
I'll sleep on the sofa
Dreaming of mother

I got a paper and read the news
Which announced the death of Suzanne Hughes
It said: this is the 2012 Run-Out Groove Blues

I scrawled "2012 RUN-OUT GROOVE BLUES" at the top of the page and it was the last song I ever wrote. I took a piece of tape and taped the sheet to my bedroom wall, and stood in front of it with my guitar strapped on and began to work out the chords to go with the melody which I'd already written in my head.

22.

The crowd parted for me as I quit the stage for the garden, and I drew a fag from the packet in my pocket and lit up, and leant against the pub's cool brick exterior. The sky was cloudless and the air was very cold, and I felt sweat crystallise on my bare arms as I stood there, shivering; I watched my breath rise from my mouth as pearlescent plumage.

"Judas Obscurus," said Astrid, suddenly appearing in the doorway. I tried to think of what to say.

"I didn't know you were coming," I said. I hadn't seen her in the audience, or at all, for a lifetime.

"Great show," she said. I said thank you. She came towards me and we briefly embraced, and it was fine. She clapped her hands on my shoulders genially and looked at me full in the face, very close, her eyes flitting from my left eye to my right, and said that she was so glad I was playing again. I said I was too, though in that moment it occurred to me that I might have just played the last show I'd ever do. Astrid lit a cigarette. I asked about the label and she told me it was going fine, they were signing new artists all the time, and it was a shame we'd lost touch. She told me that Harrison said hello, and he was sorry he couldn't make it. I said I knew everyone would be busy. Astrid nodded. Over the garden wall we could hear the sound of wet footsteps, and passing cars.

"I just wanted to say," I said then, very quickly, "about the tour–"

"Honestly, Jude," Astrid said, kindly interrupting me, but with a look of pained embarrassment that I had brought it up – I guess she thought it was obvious that we'd moved on, but

I hadn't got it. But then I did get it and when she saw me get it, she smiled and said, "It's OK." I smiled in stupid gratitude, and felt something hard in my chest slowly breaking apart. "Can I get you a drink?" she said. We were looking at each other fondly, each through our own veil of smoke.

"No thanks," I said. Astrid nodded, dropping her cigarette on the ground and crushing it underfoot. I did the same. We went back into the bar. My eyes scanned the room for Rip and I asked Marta where he was, and she told me that he'd already left.

I went to the bathroom and, while washing my hands, looked at my same old face in the mirror. I headed back to the bar, and stopped short when I saw Astrid and Marta together, and Astrid was saying something into Marta's ear. Marta turned and saw me standing there, and looked at me with a slow, half-sad smile, which I slowly returned.

•

After Mum's wake, Dad drove me to the station. He seemed not to want to talk, and I thought that that was fine. I'd fiddled with the radio and felt him shifting irritably in his seat as the road drew us to the station, and I said "oh" when I recognised a tune and Dad said "what" and I leaned towards the dash to listen closely and Dad said "what" again so I said, "it's one of mine." I'd been on the radio before, but not for a long time, and it was so strange that someone would choose to play it, and today of all days. I looked at Dad through my eyelashes, without turning my head, and said, "bet you never thought I'd be able to do something like that, did you?" He turned and looked me, taking his eyes off the road, and replied, "I never doubted that you'd get what you wanted."

Acknowledgements

Thank you Alex Coward: your irrepressible good cheer and insightful edits were the making of *Run-Out Groove* – everything of mine is yours. Thank you Frey Kwa Hawking for being the first to tell me I could do it; thank you Anna Hall, for being the first to read it. Thank you Holly Faulks for your patience and wisdom; thank you Azad Sharma and Kashif Sharma-Patel, and the whole the87press team, for giving *Run-Out Groove* a home. Thank you Geffen Semach for giving me a shot. Thank you Susan, Siri, Rachel, Jarrett, James. I love you all.